To
Gevia

Villainy at the
Village Store

Happy reading

Elizabeth Ducie

Elizabeth (Kate)

A Chudleigh Phoenix Publications Book

Cover design: Berni Stevens

Map of Coombesford: Otis Lea-Weston

ISBN: 978-1-913020-13-2

Printed by Hedgerow Print, Crediton, Devon, EX17 1ES

Chudleigh Phoenix Publications

For all my friends in the Women in Publishing community

The Village Store in Coombesford

PROLOGUE
WEDNESDAY 7TH SEPTEMBER 2022

They didn't have to get very close to the sprawled figure under the trees to see something was wrong. This may well have been a wild camper, although there was no sign of a tent or any other camping equipment, but it was clear the person in the red anorak was definitely not sleeping now. Celia Richardson gasped and grabbed her husband's arm, realising they were undoubtedly looking at a dead body. And from the angle of the arms and legs, it didn't look as if they'd died peacefully in their sleep.

"You stay here, lovey," insisted Roger, gripping his wife by both arms and pushing her gently down onto a bench by the side of the path. "I'll have a closer look."

"Oh, Roger, do be careful." Celia looked around her with a shuddering feeling they were being watched. "Maybe we should leave and call the police. What if there's someone else still here?"

"From the way the dew's soaked into that anorak, that body's been here for hours. I just want to check something first."

Celia sat with her hands held to her mouth to stop them trembling, as she watched Roger walk further along the path. He stopped, looked at the figure on the ground and then walked back. Taking her hand, he pulled her to her feet and set off towards the main path. When she tried to say something, he just shook his head and kept walking.

Once they were back by the lake, Roger pulled his phone out of his pocket and hit 999. Celia could hear the faint sounds of the call being answered and the usual question asked.

"Police, please," he said. "We've just found a body in the woods in Stover Country Park." He was silent for a few minutes, then shook his head. "No, I touched nothing, but he's definitely dead. Yes, yes, of course we'll stay here until someone arrives. My name? Richardson. Roger Richardson. I live in Coombesford." He disconnected the call, then looked across at Celia, who was trying hard not to cry.

"They said they'll be here as quickly as they can. But we're going to have to make a statement, so we could be here for a while. I'll give young Rohan a call. He has nothing major on at the moment. I'm sure he'll be willing to cover for us for a couple of hours."

After making the second call, Roger put his phone back in his pocket and sat on the bench next to Celia. He took her hand.

"How're you doing, old girl?" he asked.

"I'm okay." She tried to smile, but could feel her cheeks were stiff and knew it wouldn't fool Roger. "It's a shock, that's all, finding a dead body in such a beautiful, peaceful place. And it's a terribly undignified way to go, a stranger in a strange place." When there was no response, she looked more closely at her husband, who was staring at his toe, digging it into the sandy soil in front of the bench. She suddenly got the feeling there was something he wasn't telling her. "Roger, what is it? What's the matter?" She felt him squeeze her hand, and a sudden thought hit her. "He wasn't a stranger, was he? Roger? Roger? Oh my God, it's someone we know, isn't it?"

Roger turned to face her fully. She saw him inhale slowly, and steeled herself, knowing what he was about to say was not something she wanted to hear.

"You're going to have to be very brave, my darling," he said. "I'm afraid I do know that person. We both do." He paused and took another deep breath. "It's Stanley, Celia. It's Stanley Wentworth lying there under the trees."

CHAPTER 1
FRIDAY 19TH AUGUST 2022

The sound of a meadowlark pulled Esther Steele out of her deep concentration. She glanced out of the open window before placing her paintbrush down on the edge of the table. The tips of the bristles were quite dry, and she wondered just how long she'd been staring into space this time. When she heard the bird a second time, she laughed and reached for her phone. So that was her father's contribution to this week's 'guess the ring-tone' competition. An easy one for someone who spent all her time listening to the world around her. She was willing to bet he'd struggle more with her challenge to him, Darth Vader's march. She must ring him later to make sure he'd heard it.

"Hello, Esther Steele speaking."

"Esther, hello. It's Annie McLeod, from The Falls."

"Hi there, Annie. How's it going? How's the family?"

"They're both fine, thanks."

"That's great. You guys must come up for tea soon. And bring young Suzy with you."

"How kind. We'd love to." Esther wondered if Annie knew she wasn't just being kind. She was no great lover of her own company. She might not get out much herself, but she loved having visitors and was never happier than when sharing her cakes and biscuits around the kitchen table. The soft Scottish voice at the other end continued. "Actually, it's Suzy I'm phoning about. It's her birthday next month. She'll be eleven. And I wanted to commission one of your wonderful sketches for her."

"What a lovely idea, Annie."

"But I wanted to ask… um, please feel free to say no, if you don't think it's a good idea… but I was wondering…"

There was a silence, and Esther wondered if the signal had dropped. It wasn't like Annie to be this hesitant.

"Are you still there?"

"Yes, sorry." There was another pause before her words came out in a rush. "I wanted to ask whether you could incorporate Suzy's face into the picture in some way? It may be a daft idea. Charlie didn't think you'd consider it."

"Annie, I think it's a brilliant thought. What did you have in mind? A fairy scene, or something more dramatic? Maybe a space battle?"

"No, she's too young for that. And too ethereal. She's into fantasy rather than science fiction at the moment."

"How about a princess escaping on a dragon's back, maybe?" Esther paused and then clicked her fingers. "I've got it. Last time we spoke, you said you'd started reading Tolkien with her. How about a scene from The Prancing Pony? With Suzy as a hobbit wench helping to serve the tankards of beer? Or maybe a party in Hobbiton? Bilbo's eleventy-first birthday party!"

"That would be perfect. And so appropriate for where she's living – not that she gets behind the bar at the moment, of course, but maybe one day…"

"I've just got one request," said Esther. "If this works out well, can I pinch the idea and develop it commercially? Bespoke pictures of people in different settings?"

Annie laughed.

"You mean things like Olga as the princess escaping from a dragon?" Olga Mountjoy was a young Ukrainian woman, widow and owner of Mountjoy Manor. After a rocky start to her life in the village and the violent death of her husband, she was now settled in the community and appeared to be enjoying her role as lady of the manor. "Or Celia and Roger Richardson as caterers on a spaceship? Your dad as a cattle rancher on a steam punk Midwest ranch? Yes, I see what you mean."

"It might only be a popular idea for a short time, but I reckon it's got the potential to be quite a little money-spinner. I'll give it some thought." Esther smiled to herself as the possibilities continued to buzz around in her head. "But I'll make sure Suzy's present gets top priority. Now, have you got a recent picture of her I can use as a model?"

"I certainly have. A whole gallery of them, in fact. Shall I pop over one day this week and we can pick one together?"

"Whenever you're free. It's not like I'm going anywhere, is it?"

Arrangements made, Esther disconnected the call and dropped her phone on the workbench. She rubbed the back of her neck and winced, easing the tension with her fingers. Walking to the window, she stared across the farmyard towards the road, one arm gripping the other at her elbow. No sign of her father yet. There was a good hour before she needed to prepare supper. Plenty of time to get back to her illustration. But somehow, she didn't think she had much inspiration left.

Whistling for Frisk, her ancient companion who had long since outlived his name, she picked up her secateurs and gardening gloves and headed for the back door.

CHAPTER 2

Amelia Johnson gazed at the double page spread in the *Mid-Devon Advertiser*, lifted her chin and threw her shoulders back. If this didn't put the Village Store (proprietor Mr Stanley Wentworth) on the map, then nothing would. Regional Finalist in the Rural Service Industry Awards, no less. Who'd have thought it?

She'd spotted the notice online months ago. Stanley had been in bed with a severe case of man-flu, and the closing day for entries was coming up. So she'd written their entry all on her own. She'd had to embroider it a little, of course. Delivering the odd parcel of groceries to a pensioner during lockdown had morphed into a full 24/7 response service to the vulnerable members of the community. And in describing the items they stocked in the small grocery section as "a lifeline for anyone who was isolating", she'd conveniently forgotten to mention Cosy Corner, the much larger grocery store in the centre of Coombesford, and the full delivery service provided by Roger and Celia Richardson. But she was sure everyone else who entered had done the same. And it had obviously done the trick.

She wasn't sure why she hadn't told Stanley about entering the competition once he'd returned to work, but somehow she'd never quite got around to it. Besides, she'd reasoned, it was highly unlikely they were going to get anywhere in the contest. There was bound to be stiff competition from the other villages and towns across the county.

However, it looked as though she'd underestimated herself; or overestimated the popularity of the competition. She was going to have to tell Stanley, after all. Never mind. He rarely opened the local newspaper, so she could pick her moment, wait until he was in a good mood. She checked the date in the article. The award ceremony wasn't for another couple of months, so she'd plenty of time.

She allowed herself a brief daydream. If they won the regionals, they would move forward into the national contest. And there was a decent cash prize for the overall winners. The article listed the finalists in all the other regions too. At this moment, across the country, people would see the details of the Village Store, together with Stanley's name and photo. One in the eye for those Richardsons, that was. Stanley was definitely going to be pleased, wasn't he?

Amelia Johnson had lived in Coombesford for ten years and had worked for Stanley Wentworth since 2018, when he first opened the post office-cum-grocery store on the new estate. The pair worked well together and, if Stanley seemed oblivious to her desire to make their partnership something more than merely a business relationship, she hadn't given up hope yet. Amelia was used to playing a long game. And she knew her boss appreciated her help in promoting the new business and keeping it afloat during the rocky couple of years they'd just been through. She was the ideas person in the arrangement, and although Stanley sometimes baulked at her wilder publicity-seeking suggestions, he generally went along with her proposals. Hopefully, this time would be no different.

But in the event, it wasn't Amelia who broke the news to Stanley. When she came back from lunch that afternoon, he was standing behind the counter staring at the telephone with a thunderous look on his face.

"I've just had that young reporter from the *Mid-Devon Advertiser* on the phone," he said. "They want to do a profile of us and the Village Store? Said we're finalists in some contest or other? Apparently the organisers want to syndicate it across all the regions 'to maximise the publicity', he said." Stanley used his fingers to mime speech marks.

"Okay, right." Amelia decided she needed to take things slowly and see how the conversation went.

"I said no, obviously."

"No? Why on earth did you say no?"

"Well, I know nothing about any contest. It's obviously a scam, isn't it? They'll probably take lots of pictures and then want us to pay for an advert at the same time. Isn't that how these things work?"

Amelia smiled and shook her head.

"No, it's not a scam, not this time. I was going to tell you this afternoon. Entries for the Rural Services Awards closed while you were off sick that time, so I thought I'd have a go. I didn't think we'd get anywhere, but they've just announced the regional finalists and we're on the list." She paused and then lifted her eyebrows at him. "What do you reckon, Stanley? The ceremony's at the end of October. Shall we put on our glad rags and have a night on the town?" She stopped talking as Stanley shook his head.

"No, I'm not interested. What good is some award going to do for us? And we're far too busy to talk to reporters." He held up his hand as she opened her mouth to argue. "I'm sorry, Amelia, but it's a daft idea and a waste of time. We're not doing it. And as for maximising the publicity across the country, why on earth would we want our business plastered all over the place?" He turned abruptly away from her, stalking into the office and slamming the door.

Amelia sighed and shook her head. It looked as if she wouldn't get her night on the town after all. Although she didn't think she'd bother removing them from the nominations list. She'd just leave things as they were for now. Maybe Stanley would change his mind after he'd thought things through.

She picked up all the copies of the *Mid-Devon Advertiser* and moved them to one of the lower shelves. With a bit of luck, they'd sell out over the next couple of days and Stanley would never know his name and photos were already 'plastered all over the place', as he put it. Although why that was necessarily a bad thing, she really couldn't understand.

CHAPTER 3

"Remind me why we're spending our precious time off visiting a total stranger?"

Annie hid a smile as she looked across at Charlie Jones. She was shuffling along beside her with her hands in her pockets, scowling. Sometimes it was difficult to work out whether she was talking to her partner or to their eleven-year-old daughter.

"Amelia Johnson's not a total stranger, Charlie. She's a friend of mine." Annie paused and pulled a face. "Okay, maybe that's putting it a bit strongly. She's an acquaintance of mine. We sing in the choir together. And you must have seen her when you've been to the post office? She even drops into The Falls for a drink occasionally, although she's usually on her own and doesn't stop long. She's been in the village much longer than us, for the past ten years, I think. But she doesn't seem to have many friends. I think she's lonely. When she invited me for coffee, I didn't have the heart to say no."

"Okay. And I'm coming along because…?"

"Because it's the only way I can get to spend some time with you when we're not rushed off our feet in the bar or the restaurant kitchen." Charlie looked at her and raised one eyebrow. Annie grinned and nodded. "And yes, I suppose, because if it's too awful, you being there will help make it easier. Or more fun. Or something." She shook her head and shrugged. "I'll do your early shift tomorrow morning to say thank you," she finished, with what she hoped was a winning smile.

"Oh trust me, lady, if it's too awful, you'll be doing the morning shift for more than one day!" Charlie took the sting out of her words by putting her arm around Annie's shoulders and pulling her towards her in a quick hug. At that moment, Annie knew it was going to be all right.

The couple crossed the empty road in front of The Falls, the pub and restaurant they ran together, and turned into Hill View, passing small semi-detached houses, each pair painted in a different pastel colour. The road climbed gently, gradually turning to the right, and ended at the only old buildings on the new estate: a row of converted Devon long houses. On the ground floor were retail units comprising the Village Store, a laundrette, and a hairdresser.

"It's around the side," said Annie, leading the way past the three retail properties and down an alleyway. A stone stairway took them up to a tiny railed landing with a tub of bright orange geraniums sitting next to a black front door with a gleaming silver knocker. Annie tapped smartly, and seconds later the door flew open.

"Come in, come in. How lovely to see you, Annie. And I'm delighted you've brought Charlie. I'm so glad you could both come." The woman at the door was wearing a low-cut emerald green tee-shirt and matching sweatpants. Her flowing auburn hair fell to just below her shoulders and swung free as she continued to talk, gesticulating wildly as she ushered them into her lounge. Her skin was clear and quite pale. She was tall and well built, but without an ounce of spare fat on her. Annie thought she looked stunning, and from the look on her partner's face, so did Charlie.

As the three women stood in the sunny open-plan room, there was a brief awkward moment of silence. Annie felt the need to fill it.

12

"Amelia, this is Charlie, as you guessed. Charlie, meet Amelia Johnson, my fellow choir member."

Amelia pointed to a cream corduroy sofa pushed back against one wall.

"Sit, sit, I'll just get the tray. The kettle has boiled. Is coffee okay for both of you?"

They nodded, and she crossed to the kitchen area. It was neat and almost empty. Annie thought of their own crowded space in The Folly, their tiny house in the grounds of The Falls, and smiled ruefully to herself.

"What a beautiful room," said Charlie. "So light and airy. And I love your collection of farm animals."

Annie looked at her in surprise. It wasn't the sort of thing Charlie usually noticed or commented on. She was obviously trying with this visit, despite her earlier protestations. Amelia was beaming as she returned with a cafetière, three mugs and a plate of chocolate cookies that looked very familiar to Annie.

"Please don't tell my boss," she said, pointing to the plate. "He'll accuse me of disloyalty, but Celia Richardson's chocolate chip cookies are to die for. I often pop in for a bagful when I'm passing."

"Amelia works for Stanley Wentworth downstairs in the Village Store," Annie reminded Charlie.

"Ah, right, I understand," said Charlie with a grin. The entire village knew about the feud between the Richardsons at Cosy Corner and the proprietor of the rival store on the estate. And many people also knew it stemmed from what happened when Celia was still a teenager.

"But you were admiring the room, Charlie," Amelia went on. "Thank you. I'm really pleased with it – and with the rest of the place, for that matter. The developers did a wonderful conversion job. I'll show you around before you go if you'd like to see it?"

"That would be great," said Annie. "We just love nosing around other people's property. I used to be an estate agent in my former life. Is this your place, or is it rented?"

"Oh, it's all mine," said Amelia with a proud smile. "I did rather well out of my divorce settlement." She waved away the murmur of concern from Annie. "It was all a long time ago. We were both far too young and you know what they say about marrying in haste…" She blinked away what Annie suspected, despite her brave words, might have been a few tears. "And it allowed me to move back to this wonderful part of the world and buy this apartment all of my own. It all worked out for the best, in the end."

The three women chatted easily from then on. Annie was delighted to see Charlie relaxing on the sofa and sharing a joke with their new friend. She gazed around the room. Apart from the neat kitchen and a small round pine table and chairs, there was the seating area with the sofa and two armchairs around a small coffee table. Against the wall opposite the vast picture window was an old-fashioned glass cabinet filled with miniature animals. It was this that Charlie had commented on earlier. Annie rose and walked to look at them. In the mirror above the cabinet, she caught Amelia watching her.

"I grew up a townie," their host said, "but I've always loved the countryside ever since my friend and I helped on a farm back when we were kids. When my dad realised how much I loved animals, he bought me a model farm for my birthday." She laughed. "I was fifteen, way too old for it really, but he always threw a dollop of irony into everything he did. I carried it around with me whenever I moved house. The farm building collapsed years ago, but I still have all the animals."

Annie smiled and looked at the display which covered one entire shelf. There were three cows and a large black bull. A flock of sheep. Two geese and a couple of turkeys. And three beautiful horses. Although one of them seemed out of scale with the others. It was larger and made of metal rather than moulded plastic. She was about to comment on that when Charlie jumped up and pointed to her watch.

"Annie, look at the time! Suzy'll be home from school

and wondering where we are. And Pauline Wilson's supposed to be dropping in later to discuss the arrangements for her mother's wake."

Amelia gasped, and her hand flew to her throat.

"I didn't know Pauline's mother had died! How dreadful."

"Yes, it happened a couple of days back," said Annie. Their host had gone quite white and for a second, Annie thought she was going to faint. "Are you okay, Amelia?"

"Yes, I'm fine, thank you, Annie. It was just a bit upsetting, you know? Mrs Wilson and I used to have a chat each time Pauline brought her in to collect her pension. I didn't know she was so ill." She looked around distractedly and then picked up a pen. "I must send Pauline a note. Say how sorry I am to hear the news."

"She'd appreciate that," said Charlie. "It's not been easy for Pauline these last few years, but she's going to miss her mum now she's gone." She stood and held out her hand to Amelia. "It's been great meeting you. I'm so glad Annie suggested I come along." Annie watched, amused, as Amelia ignored Charlie's outstretched hand and pulled her into a tight hug.

"And it's great to meet you too, Charlie. Do come again soon. And we'll have that tour of the place next time, I promise."

CHAPTER 4

The motorbike was in the car park when Charlie drove back from the wholesalers. She left the Land Rover parked around the back so she could unload her supplies straight into the kitchen of The Falls–but decided she could spare a couple of minutes before she started. She strolled back around to the front and stared at the evil-looking machine resting indolently on the tarmac in front of her. Black, shiny, boxy, and with red and gold slashes on both engine covers. It was her kind of bike.

"She's a beauty, ain't she?" The voice behind her made her jump, and she spun around.

"Most impressive, yes," she replied. She paused, uncertain. He was wearing a black leather bomber jacket over his greasy tee-shirt and denim jeans, and he was carrying a motorcycle helmet, but surely this rider and this machine couldn't possibly go together. If they did, there was no justice in this world.

The figure in front of her was slight and shorter than her. His dull brown hair was very short at the sides but stuck up like a thick stiff brush across the top of his head. His skin looked as though it hadn't seen too much sunlight lately, pale and flaked. Old acne pits scarred his cheeks and his forehead. The flat tone of his voice suggested a Midlands background, certainly not the southwest. He looked hangdog and just slightly whipped; unassuming, in fact. Until you came to look at his ears. The piercing in his left earlobe carried a looped silver chain from which a small crucifix dangled. His right ear sported a thick silver and enamelled ring inside a medium-sized lobe hole. Charlie had seen larger, but even this one looked unnatural. And she knew Annie hated them with a passion. There was going to be some loud sniffing if this young man was coming in for a drink or some lunch.

And yes, the earrings were out of place on this creature, but his ride was even more so. Charlie smiled and pointed at the bike with a jerk of her head.

"How does she handle?"

"Like a swan," he said. "It seems so calm and still up top, but you just know there's so much going on down below. You a biker, then?"

"I used to be." Charlie tried to hide the tinge of sadness in her voice, but suspected she didn't fully succeed. "I had a BMW 1600 for years. Went everywhere on her. Just loved that baby. But," she paused and shrugged, "life changed. I grew up. You need to be a bit more responsible once there are other people to think about." She paused and then added with a grin, "And if I'm completely honest, as you get older, the discomfort outweighs the benefits."

"Bet you still miss the feel of wind in your face, though, don't you?"

"Oh yes. There's nothing quite like flying along a straight flat country road, or an empty motorway and watching the needle tick up past the 100 mark, is there?"

"So I've heard. Not that either of us would do that, of course."

"Definitely not."

They laughed, a shared love of illicit speed and powerful machines uniting them temporarily.

His accent was strong, and Charlie hazarded a guess.

"Have you brought her all the way from the Midlands

today?"

The smile disappeared, and for a minute he looked hunted again. She wondered if she'd scared him off and why it would matter if she had. But then he smiled and nodded at her.

"Clever lady. What gave it away? Was it the registration number on the bike? BJ is common in Birmingham. Although I'm actually from Coventry." He paused, then continued with a cheeky grin, "Can't think what else it might have been!"

"Well, let's just say you certainly don't sound like a Devonian!"

"Yes, I've been told that before." He pointed at his bike. "She's quite deceptive, really. I know she looks like a bit of a devil, but she's a great one for a beginner." Charlie raised her eyebrows, and he shook his head. "No, I'm not a beginner. I've been riding bikes since I got my licence. But I've not been on one for a while, and I don't know the roads around here, so I thought something quite gentle would be a good place to start. She only does around 47 horsepower."

"But she certainly looks harder than that."

"Oh yes, she does that." He looked around at the pub and rubbed his hands together. "Right, tell me about this place. Does it do good grub? I'm starving."

"Well, I've heard it described as the best pub in Coombesford. But I could be biased. And to be fair, it is the only pub in Coombesford. But we try our best." She winked at him and held out her hand. "I'm Charlie Jones. I run The Falls with my partner, Annie."

"Black. Rory Black," he replied. "Late of Coventry, but currently spending some time in this beautiful part of the world."

"Business or pleasure?"

"Bit of both, really. Let's just say I thought it was a good time to get out of the city and the country air does me good. But I'm also looking up an old acquaintance while I'm here."

"And are you looking for accommodation too? We've got a few rooms upstairs and one of them's available at the moment."

Rory Black shook his head.

"No, thanks. I've got digs in Teignmouth. They're not luxurious, but they'll do for the moment. If all goes according to plan, I may have somewhere much better to stay within a short while."

"That sounds intriguing."

"Let's just say an old contact of mine owes me a lot and could be very pleased to see me. I'm hoping to be welcomed with open arms." He turned towards the door of the pub. "Right, Charlie Jones, let's see whether The Falls lives up to its reputation as the best pub in Coombesford or not, shall we?" He held out his hand and gestured for her to precede him through the front door and into the bar. "But you'll have to advise me on the best ales around here. I'm a Batham's man myself. Their best bitter is legendary. Comes from a little brewery in Brierley Hill. But I don't think it ever goes much further than Brum or Coventry. I'm certainly not going to get it down here. What do you recommend?"

Charlie poured the young man a pint of Jail Ale and took it over to him, together with the bar menu. She wondered why this stranger had appeared in the village at this point in time and who this old contact of his might be? The pair could very well be in for a joyful reunion. But something in the man's tone of voice suggested that might not be the case. Charlie might have left her old life behind her, but her instincts were still keen. She decided she'd better keep an eye on Mr Rory Black.

CHAPTER 5

Hearing footsteps crossing the farmyard and entering the mud room, Esther switched on the toaster and filled each section with a slice of yesterday's bread. Today's loaves were still rising, and she'd bake them mid-morning, ready for lunchtime. In the corner Frisk raised his head from his basket, gave a welcoming whine and thumped his tail on the floor, as the kitchen door opened and an excitable younger dog raced into the room and streaked towards Esther, followed more slowly by her father.

"Good morning, Esther. Is breakfast ready? I'm starving!" Then, clicking his fingers at the young dog: "Easy, Tinker! Sit down, boy. You'll have poor Esther over if you carry on like that."

Farmer Tommy Steele had been asking the same question every morning since Esther took over running the household in her mid-teens. Nevertheless, it always gave her a warm feeling that everything was right with the world, and she felt herself smile.

"One of these days, I'm going to say 'no' to that question," she said with a laugh. "And then what would you do?"

"Oh, I wouldn't believe you, girl. I'd still wash up and sit myself at the table. I know you'd never let me down."

Esther grinned at her father and pulled a series of casserole dishes out of the warming oven, setting them on the table. She watched as he piled his plate with bacon, sausage and black pudding from a friend's pigs, eggs from their own hens, and mushrooms from the local market. Her father's appetite was prodigious, but given he'd already been out for three hours doing the milking, it wasn't surprising he was hungry.

Tommy Steele was well over six foot tall and solidly built. It was from him Esther got her own impressive stature. But unlike his blonde daughter, his hair was very dark, even now, and he had to wear it clipped short to keep his unruly curls under control. His complexion reflected the time he spent out of doors. He had a year-round tan that now, towards the end of summer, was as dark as the walnut furniture in their dining room.

Esther made herself a bacon sandwich and sat down opposite her father.

"Much on today, Dad?" she asked, passing him the tomato ketchup and watching in amusement while he liberally spread it across his food. Her father nodded, but said nothing until he'd swallowed his mouthful.

"Yes, I want to see how the stable refurbishment project is coming along. It seems to be a bit slow to me. And we're getting the pens ready for the new arrivals after next week's market."

"So how many for lunch, then?"

"Three, maybe four. I'll text you around eleven o'clock, as usual."

"That's fine. There's plenty of salad, and I made a huge gala pie yesterday, and some quiches. I've got a couple of deadlines to meet this week, so I thought I'd stock up on a few things so I could get more time in the studio for a few days."

"Sounds sensible. How's the illustrations coming along?"

"Very well. In fact, I picked up an interesting one the

21

other day. It's given me a great idea for a new product line. I'm thinking it through at the moment; I'll tell you all about it later this week."

Esther's father put down his knife and fork, wiped his plate with the last piece of toast, and cleared his throat. Esther felt her palms go sweaty, and rearranged the condiments on the table, giving her hands something to do. It had been a while, but she knew what was coming.

"I was thinking," her father said, "when I go up to North Devon next week to pick up those animals, why don't you come with me? We could go up the day before the sale, find somewhere nice to eat and stay, make a bit of a holiday out of it."

"What a lovely idea," she said, trying to inject a note of enthusiasm into her voice. "Can I check my diary and get back to you?"

From the look he gave her, she knew he knew she knew her diary was completely empty. He pushed his chair back and came round to her side of the table. His knees creaked, and he grimaced slightly as he crouched down in front of her and took her hands in his.

"Esther, darling, I'll never force you to do anything you don't want to." She bent her head and bit her lip as her eyes prickled with tears. He put a finger below her chin and gently raised her head so she was looking at him. "You know that, don't you?" She nodded as he continued. "But it's been so long since we went anywhere together. I would appreciate the company. And I think a change of scenery—"

"I'll try, Dad," she broke in. "I really will. But I've got all those illustrations to finish. I don't want to let anyone down."

"I know you don't," he whispered, releasing her hands and rising to his feet. "I've always known that." He rubbed his hands together and carried on at a more normal volume. "Right, must get on. Thanks for a lovely breakfast, as always. I'll text you later and we'll be in for lunch around one o'clock." Whistling to Tinker, he headed for the door.

Esther stood at the window, taking quick, shallow breaths and clenching her fists so hard she could feel her nails digging into her palms.

"Oh, Dad, I'm so sorry," she whispered. "I try, honestly, I do."

CHAPTER 6

"Just popping across to the post office, Annie. I'll be back soon," Charlie shouted across the bar as she headed for the door. She heard a distracted response from the kitchen that might have been 'take care' or might have been something totally different. She gave a grimace as she crossed the car park and headed for the main road. There had been intermittent power cuts that morning, something to do with the work being done by the telecoms company on the road towards Chudleigh. A whole batch of loaves and rolls had failed and Annie was having to do them again. Charlie had learned it was better to leave Annie to it when she was in this sort of mood. Although maybe an early take-away this evening before service would help.

The bright sunshine of the morning had given way to heavy black clouds, and Charlie glanced up apprehensively. Maybe she'd been rash, dashing out without a jacket. She just hoped she could get to the Village Store and back before it started raining. But as she felt a few spits and spots on her bare arms, she suspected she was going to be sadly disappointed.

As she reached the parade of shops at the top of Hill View, she glanced across to the opposite side of the road. A large silver vehicle sat in the turning to the final cul-de-sac, with its nose pointing out into the road. It was a top of the range 4x4 and there was just one occupant in the driving seat. Charlie didn't recognise the vehicle, which was unusual. There were no through roads on the estate, so the only vehicles that usually came up here belonged to residents returning after a day's work in Exeter or Newton Abbot. And she knew most of them by sight.

"Nice motor," she muttered to herself. "Must be waiting for someone in the Village Store. Or maybe the hairdresser."

There was a queue of three people at the post office counter. Stanley Wentworth was sitting in his office, talking to someone on the phone. He looked up when Charlie walked in, but turned away without acknowledging her presence. Charlie felt herself go hot and then cold. It was a while since she'd been in here and she'd just remembered why. Stanley had never made her or Annie feel welcome, unlike the rest of the retailers and most of the residents of the village. And he never came into The Falls.

Oh well, she thought, *it's only once in a blue moon*. Normally, they used the post offices in Chudleigh or Newton Abbot when they were doing their shopping, but this time she'd run out of stamps and needed to get a birthday card posted today.

Reaching the front of the queue, she brightened up when she saw who was serving behind the counter.

"Hello, Amelia, how nice to see you! Holding the fort yourself today?"

The redhead smiled back at Charlie.

"Well, it's always quiet at this time of the afternoon. And young Melanie's got Edward coming down for the weekend, so she's taken a few hours off to get the cottage ready for him."

"Yes, of course! She mentioned it when she did her babysitting shift last night. She's really excited about it, isn't she? And he gets so little time off from touring."

Melanie, another member of the choir Annie and Amelia

sang in, was part of the rota of friends who looked after Suzy on evenings when both Charlie and Annie were busy in The Falls. Her boyfriend was an internationally acclaimed opera singer. His appearances in the village were rare, but always welcome.

By the time Charlie had purchased her stamps and handed her card over for Amelia to throw into the sack behind the counter, the rain had begun. It was fairly chucking it down. But the forecast had been for short sharp showers, and Charlie guessed this one would blow itself out pretty quickly. She decided to hang around for a few minutes to see if it would ease off, rather than getting completely soaked. Strolling over to the small shelving unit of magazines, she idly flicked through some of them. Who bought these things? She had no interest in celebrity gossip, true life crime stories—she'd had enough of those in her own life—or the latest music trends. Although she had to admit the glossy one on motorcycles looked tempting.

Glancing out of the window, she found herself directly opposite the silver 4x4. The driver had switched on the windscreen wipers and was clearing the steamed-up inside of the glass with a tissue. He definitely appeared interested in the Village Store, rather than the hairdresser. Charlie looked round. She was the only one left in the place, apart from Stanley and Amelia. Whatever the driver was doing, he wasn't waiting for someone in here.

Charlie looked more closely at the figure in the vehicle. It was difficult to see through two lots of windows and an intervening rainstorm. She leaned across and wiped the glass of the shop window, which was also steaming up. The driver went still and stared straight at her for a couple of seconds. Then the engine started. There was a squeal of tyres on wet tarmac, and the car turned into Hill View and disappeared at speed.

Within moments the rain eased off and, waving to Amelia, Charlie made a dash for it. She pushed the strange car and mysterious driver to the back of her mind.

Until six o'clock that evening, that is. Charlie was behind the bar and glanced out of the window as a vehicle drove into the car park. A large vehicle. A large silver 4x4, to be precise.

The driver jumped out of the car and strolled into the bar. He was short, around five foot six at most, very slim, and neatly dressed in a black polo neck and black denim jeans. He wore smart, shiny loafers on his feet and looked to be in his early thirties. In his hand, he carried a small leather organiser, with a silver monogrammed DE on the front. He slid onto a stool opposite Charlie, smiled, and ordered a double slimline tonic with ice and a slice.

"Not seen you around here before," said Charlie, handing him his drink. "Are you sight-seeing or visiting someone in the village?"

The young man took a delicate sip of his drink and shook his head.

"Not here for pleasure," he replied, "although I can see it would be a lovely place to spend some downtime." He reached over and held out his hand to Charlie. "My name's Daniel Esposito. I'm here on business."

"Charlie Jones. I'm the co-owner of The Falls. What business are you in then, Mr Esposito?" Charlie detected a slight West Country accent, but didn't think it was Devonian.

"Please, call me Dan," he said. "And may I call you Charlie?" He took another sip. "I've driven down from Bristol to have a look round." *Bristol*, thought Charlie. *Bingo*. "My family owns a chain of Italian restaurants in Somerset, and we're hoping to expand into Devon."

"But Coombesford? I'd have thought Exeter or Plymouth would be a better bet for you."

The man shook his head.

"On the contrary, Charlie. There's lots of competition in the cities. And people go for cheap and cheerful. We aim for a different market. We specialise in Italian fine dining." He grinned at her look of surprise. "Yes, I know it sounds like a contradiction in terms. But have you ever been to Rome, Florence, or Milan?"

"Once or twice, yes."

"Well, you'll know that Italian cuisine is much more than pizza and spaghetti. The Esposito group has some of the best Italian chefs in the country working for us. And we set up small destination restaurants in out-of-the-way places."

"Places like Coombesford?"

"Precisely."

"Fair enough," said Charlie. "But Stanley Wentworth only took on the Village Store in the past few years. He's invested a lot of money. Surely he's not ready to sell it yet?"

Daniel Esposito looked at Charlie with a completely blank look on his face.

"Stanley Wentworth? Village Store? I'm sorry, Charlie, you've lost me. What are you talking about?"

"My apologies, Dan. I'm jumping to conclusions. I saw you parked outside the Village Store in that cloudburst, and I just assumed you were eyeing the place up."

He shrugged and shook his head.

"I only drove down from Bristol an hour ago. It can't be me you saw this afternoon. Sorry."

"Okay," said Charlie, "my mistake. It must have been another 4x4, just like yours."

"Well, there are quite a lot of them around. Now, can I have a look at your menu please? I fancy a bit of supper while I'm here."

Charlie handed over the menu and left Daniel Esposito to make his choice while she served someone else. But she was far from convinced. She was kicking herself for not making a note of the registration number when she was sheltering from the rain. But, there were NOT that many top class 4x4s around, not in a small village like Coombesford. And if he'd only just driven down, as he said, how did he know the rainstorm had been this afternoon? She'd not mentioned a time to him at all.

CHAPTER 7

"Wow, that was a pie and a half! Almost as good as my granny used to make. My compliments to the chef."

Charlie paused as she gathered the empty plates and dishes from the table and looked at the woman eating on her own. There was a lilt to her voice that spoke to a home on the other side of the Irish Sea. But not Dublin. This was softer, more rustic. Waterford maybe? Charlie remembered a drill sergeant she'd once had who came from Waterford. Although there'd been nothing gentle about his manner at all.

"Glad you liked it. Annie will be so pleased. I'll tell her what you said."

The woman, who'd arrived just after one-thirty, was the only remaining person in the restaurant. Her blue-black hair was swept back from her forehead, clipped in place at the crown in an old-fashioned beehive. At the back, it hung down in strands to below her shoulders. Looked at closely, she was older than her voice suggested. Her forehead had wrinkles and there were laughter lines around her mouth. Charlie guessed she'd never see forty again and might even be in her fifties. But her clothing suggested an attempt to hold back time. Her blouse was ruched and low cut, in a bright floral pattern which clashed somewhat with the bold geometrics of the tight short skirt. Her long tanned legs were bare, and she was wearing high Rocket Dog wedges.

"Would you like to see the dessert menu?" she asked. "Annie's been baking, so there's a fresh apple pie, with clotted cream or ice cream." She paused and grinned. "Or a fruit salad if you prefer something healthier?"

The woman gave a low throaty laugh and smoothed her hands over her ample hips.

"Now, do I look like I prefer healthy desserts?" she said. But then she shook her head. "Unfortunately, after that wonderful chicken and mushroom pie, I don't think I could manage one more bite. I'll just have an Americano please. Black, no sugar." She gathered up her bag and sunglasses. "And I'll take it outside, if that's okay? I like to have a ciggie after a meal. Terrible habit, I know, but," she shrugged, "no-one's perfect, are they?"

Charlie wondered for a moment if the woman was about to run off without paying for her meal. But then she concluded she wouldn't be able to run anywhere in those shoes.

"No problem. I'll bring it out," she said, pointing to the door leading to the patio and the beer garden. "And I might even join you, if I may? I allow myself just one coffee per shift, and I've got a little while before I have to clear up ready for this evening."

A few minutes later the two women sat in the sunshine, quietly sipping their coffee. Charlie's companion put down her cup and smiled.

"Now I know what a wonderful kitchen you're keeping here," she said, "I'm hoping you'll be able to rent me a room for a few days." She held out a hand, nails professionally manicured. "I'm Maureen Walsh, by the way."

"Charlie; Charlie Jones. And yes, sure we can. We've got a couple available at the moment. I'll take you up and show you when you've finished your coffee."

"It shouldn't be for too long. I'm looking up an old friend. He might offer to put me up, maybe even permanently. I understand he's come into a bit of money. And I'm very good at helping people manage their finances." She used her fingers to form inverted commas around the phrase. Then she paused and her expression changed. "But let's just say we didn't part on the best of terms. I need to mend a few fences, take things slowly."

"Sounds intriguing. I hope it all works out for you. But in the meantime, the room's free for at least the next three weeks. Take as long as you like."

"Oh, I doubt if it'll take that long," Maureen said with a laugh. "Me and Stanley go back a long way. And he always was a sucker for a pretty face and a low-cut blouse." She winked at Charlie.

"Stanley? Stanley Wentworth? That's your friend?"

"That's right. Although he's a bit more than a friend – or at least he used to be. Why? Do you know him? I understand he's taken over running a shop around here and has been doing well."

"Oh, yes. I know Stanley, although he's never been in here, as far as I can remember. He lives over the shop on the new estate, I believe." Charlie paused, uncertain how much she should say. "I'm afraid he's not too popular with all the villagers. But I wish you well with your reunion." She stood and picked up her coffee cup. "Come and find me when you're ready. I'll show you up to your room. And I'll put today's lunch on the tab, shall I?"

CHAPTER 8

When Maureen Walsh walked into the Village Store mid-morning, Stanley Wentworth was talking to a customer and didn't look up. She slipped behind a rack of newspapers and studied him over the top of her sunglasses. The years were certainly telling on him. His forehead had always been quite a high one, but now it stretched back towards the bald spot on the crown of his head. And the thin strip of hair separating the two areas of pink skin was much greyer than she'd expected it to be. He'd also put on weight, and beneath the beige store coat, his belly was straining the material of his striped shirt. But then he laughed at something his customer said and the years fell away from his face. Maureen could see once more the handsome rogue she'd fallen for so many years before. And, if she was honest, she was no longer the bright young thing she'd been in 2004. They'd met and fallen for each other at her father's annual St Patrick's Day party. She just hoped there was still some of that spark left somewhere, and that he'd give her the chance to reignite it.

At that moment, the customer picked up his bags and left. Stanley looked around the shop. He did a double take when he spotted her across the room and his face lit up.

"Maureen, sweetheart, what a lovely surprise! What are

you doing here?" He rushed across the shop and pulled her into a tight embrace. She wrapped her arms around him and allowed herself to slip back in time. Despite how it ended, she had some wonderful memories of this man.

Finally, Stanley pulled away and frowned at her.

"What's the problem? Why are you here?" He looked around. "And where's Jack?"

She'd thought long and hard about this conversation. How she played the next few minutes would affect many things, possibly the rest of her life. She lowered her eyes and squeezed out a single tear. She'd always been good at that. Stanley had never realised she could turn on the waterworks at will. Such a sucker for a damsel in distress, was her Stanley.

"I couldn't take it any longer, Stanley," she whispered, sniffing softly. "He was good to me at first, but then everything changed. He became a different man; so cruel. And then he hit me!"

"What? Jack Windsor? Never! He's not that sort of man."

Maureen smiled at him, aiming for somewhere between wistful and heartbroken.

"You wouldn't think so, would you, Stanley?" She paused, waiting for him to catch up. "But then you never thought he was the sort of man to run off with your wife, now did you?"

"True. Very true. But I can't believe he hit you. Wait until I get my hands on him! I'll kill him!"

Maureen shook her head.

"No, don't say that, Stanley. I couldn't bear it if you got into trouble for me. It only happened the once. And he was sorry afterwards. Swore he'd never do it again. But that's what they always say. And I didn't hang around and give him the chance to break his word. I scraped together a bit of money and as soon as I got the opportunity, I ran away and left him." She paused, then stretched out her hand and rested it gently on his arm, purple-coated nails gently scratching at the material of his coat. "I don't want him to know where I am, Stanley. You must promise me you won't go after him."

Maureen could see this was a lot for Stanley to take in. But then life with her had never been smooth sailing, had it? It had been a shock when he found out his wife was carrying on with his best friend. And an even greater shock when, having offered to forgive her and take her back, he was told she didn't want or need his forgiveness. She was off to spend her life with the younger, richer man.

They'd parted more in sorrow than anything else, at least on his part, and had kept in touch occasionally in the years that followed. And now to find out he'd left his wife in the hands of a man who turned out to be violent. Maureen could see Stanley was finding it all difficult to take in. Maybe this was the time to give him the rest of the picture while he was off balance.

"And even before he hit me, things weren't going well. The worse he got, the more I realised how much of a mistake I'd made!" She sighed and squeezed out another tear. "I was such a fool, Stanley. I had a man who truly loved me; a good man. And I threw it all away for a bit of glamour. But you know what they say about all that glitters not being gold..."

"Glisters."

"What, dear?"

"It's glisters, not glitters. All that glisters is not gold. Common mistake, everyone makes it."

She felt a tiny scream inside her head. She'd forgotten how pedantic he could be, and how he always had to show off his education by being smart and correcting her. But that was a small price to pay for a safe haven until she found something better.

And of course, she had no genuine worry about Jack Windsor coming to find her. She hadn't left him. Quite the opposite. He'd walked out on her. Sent her a text saying he'd left the country! He was on his way to a new life in Cape

Town with his South African girlfriend. A girlfriend Maureen later found out was fifteen years younger than her, had been working in Jack's bar for eight months, although none of their 'friends' had warned her about her, and was expecting a baby. No, she very much doubted if she would ever see Jack Windsor again.

"Where are you staying? Exeter? Newton Abbot?" Stanley's question broke across her thoughts.

"No. I'm staying right here in Coombesford. I took a room at The Falls. Nice couple, Charlie and Annie. And young Suzy is delightful." Maureen could never resist teasing Stanley. She knew he was old-fashioned about things like that. And sure enough, she saw his face darken.

"Oh, I don't think that's appropriate. We can't have you staying there. I understand it's quite basic, although the food's not bad, apparently. Would you not be more comfortable in somewhere a bit more luxurious? I know some fantastic places in Exeter. Or maybe up on Dartmoor?" He paused. "How long are you planning on staying, anyway? If you want to make it long-term, we'll have to find you somewhere to rent. I can help with the money if it's a problem."

Maureen watched as his gaze roamed over the neat little store. Yes, Stanley Wentworth seemed to be doing well for himself. But she had to wonder about the stunning redhead sitting behind the post office counter tucked into the corner. She was too far away to hear their conversation, but was obviously trying to work out what was going on. Time to break a bit more news to Stanley.

"Well, yes, I told Charlie I only wanted the room for a few days. I was rather hoping I could move in with you, Stanley."

His sudden stillness told her she'd confounded him once again. Oh dear. Maybe this wouldn't be as easy as she thought.

"Oh, I don't think that would work, Maureen sweetheart. I only have a small place."

35

"I thought you lived in the enormous apartment above here?"

"Who told you that?" He paused. "Oh yes, Charlie, I suppose. Well, yes, I do. But it's not that big, and there's only one bedroom, I'm afraid. I turned the box room into an office. I don't even have a spare bed."

Maureen reached up and stroked his cheek, smiling seductively at him.

"We've only ever needed one bed before, Stanley. Why would we need two now?"

Stanley went bright pink and seemed to have difficulty speaking. He took her arm and walked her right to the end of the store, as far away from the post office counter as possible. Eventually he croaked out the words, "But that was years ago, Maureen. We're no longer married. It took me a long time to get over you. I don't think—"

"But that's where you're wrong, Stanley Wentworth." Maureen let him see her true face for a brief second before resuming her kittenish tone, almost purring at him. "You may have signed the divorce papers and sent them off to the solicitor, but I never did. And there's absolutely no reason Mr and Mrs Stanley Wentworth shouldn't be sharing a bedroom, now is there?"

She sauntered away, leaving him open-mouthed. At the door, she stopped and smiled over her shoulder at him. "I'm going to pop back to The Falls to have some lunch. I'll come back after you've closed the store for the day. Then we can have a drink and catch up on everything that's been happening lately." She blew a kiss at him. "See you later, Stanley."

CHAPTER 9

Amelia glanced at the clock on the wall behind the post office counter. Twenty past four. She sighed. More than an hour to go. She was so tired, and really needed to get some extra sleep. She hoped Stanley wouldn't invite her up to his apartment for a drink after work. He'd done that once or twice lately, when they'd been on duty together. Normally, she jumped at the chance to spend more time with him. After all, that was the reason she was working in the Village Store, wasn't it? But today was different. She really didn't have it in her to be sociable this evening. And she wanted a chance to think about the dark-haired woman whose visit had so unsettled Stanley that morning.

The bell pinged as the door opened. Amelia's eyes turned first to the shiny silver 4x4 parked immediately outside the door, and then to its owner, who had just entered. A short, slim Mediterranean-looking man with straight greased hair, he was dressed all in black, including a long unbuttoned leather coat that flapped around his ankles as he moved.

"Can I help you, sir?" said Amelia as the young man stood just inside the doorway, looking around. At the sound of her voice, Stanley looked up from where he was checking some paperwork in the office. Amelia saw him glance in the mirror, carefully positioned so he could see the whole of the shop without being seen. In theory, it was to alert him if the shop got too busy for the staff on duty, so he could come and help them. In reality, Amelia knew he used it to decide when it was prudent to appear in the shop itself and when he needed to hide. Last week, when old Mr Withers had engaged her and Melanie for nearly fifteen minutes with stories of his brilliant granddaughter, despite a queue of waiting customers, Stanley had hidden in the back until the coast was clear.

But now, his reaction was completely unexpected. He glanced at the mirror, looked away, and then looked back again. Jumping to his feet, he rushed out into the store.

"It's all right, Amelia. I'll deal with this. I know you wanted to get on with that filing in the office."

"Filing? What filing?" Amelia never went near the filing. It was something Stanley always did himself, together with most of the paperwork. But her boss, ashen-faced and sweating, was frowning at her and pointing into the office. She shrugged her shoulders and left him at the counter on his own, facing the young man.

She threw herself into Stanley's chair and leaned back with a sigh, briefly closing her eyes. So tired; she really needed to get some decent sleep tonight. If Stanley wanted her out of the way—and that much was obvious—she wouldn't argue. Maybe she could have a little rest until it was time to pack up and go home. Although she somehow doubted Stanley would let her get away with that.

She pulled the chair around so she was invisible from the shop itself, while keeping the mirror in full sight. That way, she'd be able to see if anyone else came in and needed serving. Stanley and the stranger were facing each other across the counter. Stanley was leaning heavily on the pile of local newspapers Amelia had been setting out when her boss sent her to the office. He had lowered his head and looked like an angry turkey cock. His visitor was standing with his feet wide apart and a faint, enigmatic smile on his face, slapping the back of his black leather-gloved right hand into his left palm. It was slow, rhythmic—and one of the most menacing things Amelia had seen in a long time.

The sound of their voices was a low hum, and she couldn't work out what they were saying. Then, suddenly, Stanley's voice raised.

"I need more time," Amelia heard him say. She saw him look over towards the office door. She turned and picked up the copy of the newspaper she'd brought into the office with her. Flicking it open, she paused at the obituary page. It was a feature she rarely read. She'd never understood the attraction of reading about other people's misfortune, especially total strangers. But this time, she knew there was a name she'd recognise. And according to Charlie and Annie, Mrs Wilson's funeral was going to be a big event.

At that moment, Stanley strode in.

"Everything okay, boss?" she asked, looking at him innocently, and not as though she'd been watching them in the mirror.

"Yes, yes, Amelia. Everything's fine. Daniel's an old friend of mine. Not seen him for a while."

Well, it didn't look friendly to her, but Amelia kept her thoughts to herself.

"Look, you get off home," said Stanley. "I'll finish up here. Dan and I will probably make a night of it."

Amelia stared at her boss in amazement. In the time she'd been working for him, he'd never sent her home early or given her any extra time off for anything. She'd even had to work through the special Bank Holiday for the Queen's Platinum Jubilee.

"Well, go on, what are you waiting for?" he said now. She picked up her bag from the cupboard behind the door and nodded at him.

"Okay, Stanley, thanks very much." She paused, still not convinced everything was all right, despite her boss's assurances. But he held the door open for her and waved her away. Shrugging her shoulders, she walked to the front door. Glancing back as she left, she could see the two men were deep in conversation once more. She still couldn't hear what they were saying. But one thing she was sure of: this didn't look like a reunion of old friends. As she reached the end of the parade of shops, she stopped outside the hairdresser and pulled her phone out of her bag. Opening her camera, she took a couple of snaps of the silver 4x4, and especially of the registration number. She wasn't sure why she did that. It just felt like a good thing to do. Just in case.

CHAPTER 10

"Any news from the village today?" It was another of her father's stock phrases. And a question she looked forward to answering each evening as they sat with their post-supper coffee. Esther may not have left Foster's Farm more than a handful of times in recent years, but her network was extensive. She spoke to either Annie or Charlie most days. Celia often dropped in to pick up eggs for the next day's baking. And she regularly quizzed the farmhands when they popped in to refill their flasks during the day. Plus, she was an avid contributor to *Spotted Coombesford*.

"I had quite a long talk with Pauline Wilson today. It sounds like her mother's funeral is going to be quite an event."

"Oh yes, I'd forgotten about that. Next week, isn't it?" He paused, took a sip of coffee, and then continued. "Do you want to go?"

Esther felt her heart thud. She'd wondered if he'd suggest it. She'd even persuaded herself she needed to go, to support her friend, but when it came to it, would she be able to?

"Yes, I think so. Only the service, of course. They're holding the wake in The Falls, but it's going to be packed. I can't go there." She took a deep breath, let it out slowly and smiled across at her father. "Yes, that would be good. And I think Pauline would appreciate it."

"You won't remember her father's funeral, of course. It was while you were in the hospital. Such a tragedy, that tractor turning over on him like that. The entire village turned out for that one, too."

"Oh, that's good to hear. Must have been terrible for both of them."

"Well, I'm sure there were a few rubberneckers who were there just to see the tragic widow and her young daughter. But in the main, people were genuinely heartbroken for them."

Esther held up the coffeepot and raised her eyebrow at her father. When he smiled and shook his head, she gathered the dirty mugs and took them to the dishwasher. Turning, she leaned back against the work surface and crossed her arms.

"I seem to remember our two families were friendly before all that happened. And Pauline came to visit me a few times after I came out of the coma. But we gradually drifted apart. I wonder why?"

Her father shrugged.

"It was all too much for both of us, I think. Pauline's mum had suffered a terrible loss, and was bringing up her daughter on her own. Then your mum disappeared, and it left me in the similar situation. We tried to get together a couple of times, for your sake and Pauline's. But it just brought back too many memories. So after a while, we just stopped trying. And as the years went on, it was easier to do nothing. But I'm sorry I didn't have a chance to say goodbye to her. I think I'll go to the funeral, even if you decide you're not up to it." He rose and walked across to kiss Esther on the top of her head. "Right, I've got a bit of paperwork to do. I'll see you at ten for the news?" He headed for the door. "Lovely supper, as always, Esther. Thank you."

CHAPTER 11

"Sure, that was another smashing meal, Charlie. Is Annie on duty tonight?" Maureen Walsh had been late coming into the restaurant and was the last to finish her meal.

"She certainly is, Maureen. And there's nothing to beat one of Annie's quiches for a light evening meal. I've never tasted pastry quite like hers."

"And the dressing on that salad was sublime. Do you know what she puts in it?"

"I do indeed. But I am afraid it's a family secret, handed down from Scottish grandmother to mother to daughter. If I told you, I'd have to kill you. And Annie would certainly kill me." She grinned to take the edge off her words. Nevertheless, there was no way Maureen Walsh—or anyone else—was going to find out from her how Annie made her salad dressing taste that bit better than anything you'd ever tasted before. "Do you have room for some dessert? We have a wonderful summer pudding with double cream; fresh fruit salad; or home-made ice cream."

Maureen bit her lip, then shook her head.

"No, I'm going to pass, Charlie. Otherwise, by the time I leave here none of my clothes are going to fit me. I'll just have a double espresso, please."

"And I suppose you wouldn't want one of those little

Belgian biscuits with the coffee, now would you?" Charlie looked teasingly at the other woman.

"Well, if one of those were to turn up on the saucer, it would be rude to turn it down, now wouldn't it?"

Charlie hurried back with the coffee and Speculoos. Maureen waved away the proffered sugar bowl, but unwrapped the biscuit and dipped it into her coffee.

"So, Maureen," said Charlie, busying herself tidying up one of the other tables. "How was your day? Did you get your business fixed okay?"

Maureen shook her head and pushed out her lower lip.

"I didn't get as far as I hoped, to be honest, Charlie. I went to see Stanley this morning, and we started to catch up on what's been going on since we last met. We arranged for me to go back there this evening and I really thought everything was going to be fine. But he wasn't there! He stood me up." She smiled weakly at Charlie, who wondered if Maureen was just putting on a brave face. "But it's a minor setback; just a minor setback. I'm hoping one more meeting is all it'll take and then everything will be on track. With a bit of luck, I should be out of your hair by this time next week." She paused. "Mind you, I'm going to miss Annie's cooking."

Maureen made quick work of her coffee. Charlie had never understood the attraction of an espresso, or even a double espresso. One gulp and it was gone. She much preferred a full mug that she could take her time over and savour. But they seemed to be popular. Annie had persuaded her to invest in an espresso machine after they'd had to disappoint a diner for the third time in a row. And she had to admit the thing was in constant use. She shook her head. Just no accounting for taste.

The Irish woman gathered her things together, pulling a light shawl around her and slinging the strap of her handbag over her shoulder.

"Are you off up then, Maureen?" asked Charlie. "Do you want a wake-up call in the morning?"

Maureen laughed.

"No thank you. This is a holiday; I don't have to get up early. But I'll make sure I'm down before you clear away the breakfast buffet. I missed it completely this morning. Ten o'clock, isn't it?"

"There or thereabouts, yes."

"Right-oh. But I need some fresh air after all that food. I can't just go straight to bed. I'm going out for a quick stroll. Just as far as the viewing point and back, I think. Don't worry. I'll be back long before you lock the door." She paused. "And I might even treat myself to a nightcap before I hit the sack. But only the one, mind you. I'll need a clear head when I go back to see Stanley Wentworth tomorrow morning. It looks like the soft soap didn't work, so I may be in for some hard bargaining." With a wink, she headed for the door.

"What was that all about?" The soft voice made Charlie jump. She'd not noticed Amelia Johnson sitting in the shadows at the end of the bar. "Did I hear her mention Mr Wentworth's name?"

"Er, yes, I think you did." Charlie thought quickly. The Falls was a hub in the village, along with Cosy Corner. Charlie and Annie had found the continual exchange of gossip to be useful to them in the past. But they were careful to make sure they only listened. They did as little of the talking as possible. "But I'm afraid I can't tell you what she was talking about." Well, that was the truth, thought Charlie. She hadn't said she didn't know; just that she couldn't say.

Amelia gave a sniff.

"Well, I hope she won't make a nuisance of herself. She came in this morning and the boss didn't seem pleased to see her. He's a very busy man, is Mr Wentworth. And he's got enough stress in his life already. I wouldn't like to see him being upset by some woman who's breezed in from nowhere." She swallowed the rest of her white wine spritzer in one go and pushed the empty glass across the bar. "Thanks, Charlie. That was lovely."

"Another?"

"No, I don't think so. I think I'm going to see if I can catch up with our Irish visitor and find out what she's up to." And with a wave of her hand, she headed out of the door and across the car park. Through the open door, Charlie could see it was getting dark.

CHAPTER 12

Maureen stood at the entrance to the car park and gazed westward. She watched the sun sink gently down behind the nearby hills, then turned away and headed towards the village green. She'd been born in the west of Ireland, in a small rural community, and although the family had moved to England many years before and she'd spent much of her life in towns and cities, she'd always felt at home in the countryside.

She hurried across the village green, past the churchyard. Turning right into Manor Lane, she strode out up the hill. Charlie had mentioned earlier there was a viewing point at the top of the lane, just before the gates to Mountjoy Manor. And sure enough, she soon found a bench on a semicircle of neatly mowed grass on the side of the lane, where a gap in the hedge revealed the whole of the valley. In the distance, she could see Hay Tor and other hilltops on Dartmoor. And from here, she could see the sun once again, although it wouldn't be long before it finally set for the night.

Maureen threw herself down on the bench and stretched her legs. Lighting a cigarette, she inhaled deeply and let out a long trail of smoke. She could get used to this place, she really could.

Hearing a sound behind her, she turned to look over her shoulder. A woman with striking red hair was standing on the other side of the lane. She looked familiar, and Maureen remembered she'd noticed her drinking in the bar when she'd been chatting to Charlie.

"Oh, hello," she said. "You made me jump. Where did you spring from?"

"Just out for a stroll, like you," was the somewhat surly response.

"Didn't I see you in The Falls just now?"

The other woman nodded. She was chewing a thumbnail and staring at Maureen in silence.

"Beautiful view, isn't it? Do you live around here?" Maureen was feeling uncomfortable under the silent gaze and thought it would help if she could engage the other woman in conversation. Finally, the redhead came and perched on the other end of the bench.

"Why do you want to talk to Stan...Mr Wentworth?"

Maureen felt her hackles rising, and she arched an eyebrow at her interrogator.

"I don't see how that's any of your business, do you?"

"But I'm making it my business! Why do you want to see him?"

"I'm sorry, but I don't understand why you should be concerned about Stanley?"

"Well, I work for Mr Wentworth and he's been very good to me. I don't want him upset."

"But why would you think I'm going to upset him? You don't even know me!"

"You came into the shop today." Maureen suddenly remembered the other time she'd seen that red hair–behind the post office counter. "And when you left, Mr Wentworth didn't seem thrilled. Does he know you?"

"Oh yes, believe me, he knows me. He knows me very well indeed. After all, we've been married for the best part of twenty years!" And stubbing out her cigarette and popping the butt into her pocket, Maureen stood up and

48

walked away without a backward look. She had a sneaking suspicion she was going to regret letting slip that piece of information, but she didn't appreciate Stanley's employee trying to interfere in her business.

CHAPTER 13

It was nearly eleven and Amelia was about to go to bed when she heard a thud, followed by a string of curses from outside her apartment. Switching her hall light off and grabbing her heavy torch, just in case she needed to protect herself, she eased open her front door.

During the conversion the developers had installed two stairways connected by an ornate railed walkway, providing access to all three apartments from either end of the row of buildings. Thus, Amelia had a clear view from her front door to Stanley's.

And it was her boss she could see now. He appeared to be having trouble opening his front door, as he stood swaying slightly and stabbing the key in the general direction of the keyhole.

"Having trouble, Stanley? Can I help?" she called gently. She pulled her door to, but left it on the latch, then went to join him.

He turned and blinked slowly at her.

"Can't get the key to work…" She recoiled slightly and held her breath against the strong odours of curry and beer.

"Here, let me." She took the key from his sweaty hand, opened the door, and half-pushed him inside. Stanley dropped onto the sofa and belched softly before putting his head back, closing his eyes, and starting to snore.

Amelia put her hands on her hips and shook her head.

"Oh, Stanley. Look at the state of you." There was no response, and she gave a little laugh. "Right, time to put the kettle on, I reckon."

Returning a few minutes later with a tray and two filled mugs—coffee for him, chamomile tea for her—she found he hadn't moved. Putting down the tray, she shook him, gently at first, then harder, until eventually he opened his eyes and sat up. She waited until he'd lifted his mug and taken a first sip before relaxing enough to sit opposite him.

"This isn't like you, Stanley. What's got into you? Did that Daniel lead you astray?"

"Daniel? What's he got to do with anything?"

"I thought you said you were making a night of it with him?"

Stanley stared at her, his forehead crinkled. She wondered if he was trying to remember who Daniel was, or coming up with a plausible story.

"Oh, yes, that's right. No, he had to cry off in the end. I've been into Newton on my own for a curry." He grinned ruefully at her. "Might have had one too many beers to cool down the vindaloo."

"Well, I hope you didn't drive yourself?"

"Of course not. I got a lift there and a taxi back." He stared at his coffee for a while before looking up at her. "Sorry if I disturbed you. You're right; it's not like me. I've just got a lot on my mind at the moment and I think it all got too much for me."

Amelia wondered how far she would get if she asked a few questions, then decided she had nothing to lose. Chances were he wouldn't remember this conversation in the morning, anyway.

"Who is this Daniel Esposito, anyway, Stanley? You said he was an old friend, but you didn't seem too pleased to see him."

There was a long silence. Stanley's eyes were closed and

Amelia wondered if he'd fallen asleep once more. She was about to give up and head back home when he opened his eyes and sat up.

"I've known Dan for a long time, Amelia. He's from a different place and an earlier part of my life. Let's just say I owe him big time and he's come to collect."

"That doesn't sound too good, boss. Is there anything I can do to help?"

Stanley smiled at her and shook his head.

"That's very sweet of you, Amelia, but I've got it sorted. It's just going to cost a lot of money and a bit of time. Patience was never one of Daniel Esposito's better qualities. But we came to an agreement in the end. Nothing for you to worry about."

"And that Irish woman? Is she part of it, too?"

"Maureen? Oh no, she's a different kettle of fish altogether." He rubbed his hands over his face and across the back of his neck. "To be honest, I'm not really sure what I'm going to do about Maureen."

"Not been a wonderful day, for you, has it, Stanley?"

"You could say that. In fact, I can't work out why people have suddenly started popping up from my past now. It's very strange."

Amelia suddenly felt a heaviness in her stomach. That damn article. She'd been so proud of it. But it was looking like a major mistake. She just hoped Stanley wouldn't remember she'd entered them in the competition. Tomorrow morning, she'd phone the newspaper and withdraw their nomination.

Glancing at the clock, she picked up the empty mugs and took them back to the kitchen. When she returned, Stanley was snoring again. She tapped him on his shoulder.

"Stanley, are you going to be okay? It's after midnight, and we both need our beds."

He nodded and smiled at her.

"Yes, I'll be fine. I'll just sit here for a little while. But don't worry; I won't stay here all night." She didn't believe him, but that was up to him. And she doubted it would be the first time Stanley Wentworth had spent the night asleep on the sofa.

As she reached the door, his voice, already rough with sleep, stopped her.

"You're a good friend, Amelia. I hope you know how much I appreciate you." He yawned deeply. "You know, ever since I've known you, you've reminded me of someone. Can't think who it is. But it'll come to me one of these days. Goodnight, Amelia. See you in the morning."

"Good night, boss," she whispered. "Sleep tight."

CHAPTER 14

A mist rose gently from the surface of the lake and drifted towards the trees. A waning sun peeped through the black silhouettes of the silver birch and pine trees on the distant shore. The only sound was the occasional cry of a solitary coot floating on the water in the distance. Stanley Wentworth gave a sigh of pure pleasure. He tiptoed to the water's edge, reached into his pocket, and pulled out a small plastic bag. The silence disintegrated as all hell broke loose. Supper had arrived for the birds of Stover Park.

The mallards and pochards were the first to realise what was going on. Their cacophony alerted the coots and moorhens. Next, the mandarins arrived, quarrelsome and pompous. Seagulls flew around, hoping to grab stray seeds in mid-air. And finally, from across the lake came the swans. A pair of adults, residents of several years, and this season's clutch of cygnets. Seven this time, they were three months old and already losing their cute chick appearance and moving into the awkward teenage stage.

In a few minutes the bag was empty, and Stanley continued strolling around the lake. This early evening outing had become a habit during the first lockdown in 2020. In those days, it was a chance to get out of the apartment and stretch his legs after the isolation of the day.

He'd walked quite fast and sometimes circled the lake two or even three times. Two years on, it was less of an exercise routine and more of an opportunity to spend some time alone after the bustle of a day in the Village Store.

His walk took him past the bird hide, over the bridge and along the side of the lake until he reached Squirrel Junction. That wasn't the official name, of course, but it seemed perfect for the aerial walkway among the treetops. He walked up the ramp, pausing to stare out over the hidden pond, so still it was hard to believe anything lived in it. Although if you were really lucky, you could see an occasional moorhen rooting in the undergrowth at the muddy edge. At the top of the slope, he leaned on the railing and gazed down at the forest floor twenty feet below.

"Three, four, five," counted Stanley out loud, as he watched the small grey bodies flash in and out of the undergrowth. "Only five today." Then he spotted a movement from the corner of his eye. "No, it's six. There's another one over there behind the tree stump. I can just see its tail flicking."

Stanley felt his usual urge to get closer to the squirrels. He'd fed the birds, but there was another small bag of seed in his pocket. In the main part of the park, there were always too many people around, and the squirrels rarely came close enough for him to feed them. But he knew, if he slipped through the locked gate that wasn't locked if you knew how to handle it, and crept along the hidden track behind the glade under the aerial walkway, and if he sat very still, the squirrels would come to him.

He strolled off the walkway and continued along the side of the lake. At the top, he checked to make sure there was no-one watching him, then turned quickly up the little-used pathway. Just as he reached the gate, he heard a rustle in the undergrowth behind him.

He spun around, heart pounding. Surely there were no wardens around this late. But when he saw who was standing behind him, he gave a shaky laugh and pressed a hand to his heart.

"Oh, you made me jump," he said. "What a surprise. I didn't know you'd be here tonight."

CHAPTER 15

Roger held tightly on to Celia's hand, but stared out over the lake, giving her time to compose herself. He could feel the shudders going through her and hear the quiet sobs she tried to suppress.

"Let it all out, lass," he whispered. "Let it all out."

Stanley Wentworth had been a thorn in Roger's side twice already in their lives. As a teenager he'd watched the brash newcomer, four years their senior, breeze into the village and steal his beloved Celia from under his nose. He'd endured the sight of their short courtship; the way Celia, previously so sensible, smart and with her eyes firmly set on university, had thrown it all in for love. He'd gritted his teeth and added his congratulations to everyone else's when the happy couple got engaged. And he'd picked up the pieces when just weeks before the wedding the bridegroom disappeared without trace, leaving behind a much chastened Celia who'd hidden away for months before venturing back into the café and the public eye.

And just three years previously, he'd watched on the side-lines as Wentworth, stouter, balding but as brash as ever, had arrived back in Coombesford and not only taken over running the store on the new estate in direct competition to Cosy Corner, but also blatantly tried to rekindle his relationship with Celia. Despite his head, and all his friends, telling him Celia was a devoted wife who wouldn't consider making the same mistake twice, his heart had refused to listen, and he'd spent an agonising time watching Celia grow pensive and, to his eyes, full of longing. After spotting the pair talking earnestly together one day, Roger had finally tackled his wife to find out what was going on. To his relief, she'd laughed, hugged him, and told him that while Stanley was interested in turning back the clock, she certainly wasn't and had told her former fiancé in no uncertain terms to leave her alone. Such had been Roger's relief he'd taken with equanimity Wentworth's attempts ever since to undermine the success of Cosy Corner. Although the effects of Covid and the various lockdowns had been far more effective in disrupting their business than any competitor might be.

So Roger certainly had no reason to mourn the man whose body they'd discovered under the trees. Yet, as Celia wiped her eyes, gave a deep sigh and smiled up at him, he realised his principal feeling was regret. No matter what problems he'd had with Stanley Wentworth, he knew there was no dignity attached to ending up dead under a tree in the country park. What a way to go! Roger squeezed his wife's hand, and the couple sat in contemplative silence until the sound of sirens shattered the early morning peace.

The couple walked back to the car park as a police car pulled off the road and parked next to their battered Ford Fiesta hatchback. Two constables climbed out.

"Mr Richardson? You called 999? Reported a body in the woods?" asked the driver, a rangy man with curly hair and ruddy skin. He pushed his hat onto his curls as he walked towards them.

"Yes, I'm Roger Richardson and this is my wife, Celia. It's Stanley Wentworth who runs the Village Store in Coombesford. He's on the other side of the lake. I'll take you there." He glanced at their vehicle. "There's a track over there, but I'm not sure how to reach it in the car."

"That's okay, Mr Richardson. We'll go on foot for now. We've alerted the rangers and once they arrive, we can sort out access for the vehicles."

"It's this way then," said Roger, turning back towards the lake. But Celia pulled on his arm and shook her head.

"I'll stay here," she said in a tiny voice. Not one her customers would have recognised from the cheerful, noisy woman who ruled the roost over the Coombesford café. "I don't want to see him again."

"That's alright, Mrs Richardson," said the second officer, a tiny, dark-haired woman, a few years older than her colleague. "I'm Constable Zhang. You can call me Fen. May I call you Celia? Why don't we sit in the car for a bit while Mr Richardson shows PC Ryan what you found?"

CHAPTER 16

By the time the police had secured the site, called in the Medical Examiner and the scenes of crime officers, and were ready for a preliminary chat with Roger and Celia, it was mid-morning. The car park was filling up and Celia felt curious eyes boring into her as families with pre-school children, dog walkers, bird watchers, and joggers left their vehicles and headed into the park. As the body was in an area closed to the public, the police had agreed with the rangers it was unnecessary to close the park completely, although they taped off the aerial walkway to reduce prying eyes and allow the police to work in privacy.

While Celia remained in the squad car with PC Zhang, Roger climbed into his own car, accompanied once more by PC Ryan. Celia assumed they would check their stories independently to make sure they agreed.

"So, Celia, tell me in your own words, what alerted you to the body in the woods? It was quite some way from the walkway. You must have very good eyesight."

"Well," Celia began, "we've been coming here most days for the past couple of years. It's such a nice place to walk and close to Coombesford. So I was used to the view. Usually, I take little notice of the undergrowth. But today, something was different." She paused and thought hard.

What had alerted her to the body in the woods? "It was the anorak, you see. I couldn't see much from the walkway, but there was this patch of red in the distance. Then, when I looked through Roger's binoculars, I could see it was a person. And even from a distance, it didn't look right. I felt we had to check, even if it just turned out to be a wild camper as Roger thought it was."

PC Zhang looked up as her colleague left Roger in his own vehicle and walked back towards the squad car.

"Okay, Celia, it looks like my colleague has finished talking to Mr Richardson. We've got all we need for now. We'll let you get back home and we'll be in touch if there's anything else we need to ask you."

Back at Cosy Corner, Celia was relieved to hear Rohan Banerjee was coping very well with the trade in the café. He'd not opened the grocery counter as well, but he told them most people had been quite happy to have a coffee and cake instead, and would be back later for their groceries. Rohan agreed to stay for the rest of the day, so while Roger bustled about behind the grocery store waiting for the promised rush of returning customers, Celia left the two men to it and retired upstairs to the flat.

She'd have to get some baking done later on. She knew this village well. Once news of their discovery got out – and it would get out quickly – they'd find trade was very good as people 'just happened to be passing' and popped in for coffee, cake and a dose of local gossip. And it wouldn't do to run out of cakes and scones on a busy day.

But for now, she needed a few minutes to herself.

She'd destroyed all her physical reminders of Stanley Wentworth when he jilted her so many years ago. And she certainly had nothing to remind her of his older self. But she couldn't destroy her memories. As she sat on the sofa with a pot of peppermint tea beside her and Sandy, their three-year-old ginger tom, curled up on her lap, she closed her eyes and thought back to those early days. Stanley had been such good company at first. She'd never for one moment regretted the way her life had turned out, and she loved Roger dearly, but she'd be lying if she said there wasn't a tiny part of her that wondered where she'd be today if Stanley Wentworth hadn't disappeared that day back in 1996.

It was around seven o'clock that evening. Roger had closed up the grocery store, topped up all the bulk containers ready for the following day's trade and was sitting at the table in the window with a mug of coffee, flicking through the local paper while Celia bustled around in the downstairs kitchen. Delicious aromas filled the air. Two fluffy golden sponge cakes were cooling on the racks, ready to be filled with cream and jam. A batch of cheese scones were currently rising in the oven, and Celia was rolling out the dough for her famous chocolate chip cookies. A sharp rap on the window made them both look up. Roger unlocked and opened the door.

"DCI Harolds, DS Smith. This is a surprise. Come on in." He gestured for the pair to join him at the table. "Would you like some coffee?"

"Not this evening, thank you, Mr Richardson. We just wanted a bit of a chat about this morning's discovery in Stover Park."

Celia dropped her rolling pin and gasped.

"You're still with the murder team, aren't you? Why are you involved? We thought it was natural causes, a heart attack or something."

"I'm sorry, Mrs Richardson, but we really don't think it was natural causes." Detective Chief Inspector Andrea Harolds shook her head. "We're waiting on the medical examiner's results, but we're expecting him to find evidence of poison in the stomach contents. We're treating Mr Wentworth's death as suspicious." She glanced across at her sergeant. "DS Smith, can you stay here and talk to Mrs Richardson? I can see she needs to remain near the oven at the moment. Mr Richardson, can we go up to your flat and have a chat?" She paused. "And afterwards, maybe we'll take you up on that offer of coffee after all–just so long as we can try some of those beautiful cookies."

Celia answered all the sergeant's questions quietly and firmly. Yes, she knew Stanley Wentworth. Yes, it was true they'd been engaged many years ago, but he'd let her down at the last minute. Yes, they knew he'd returned to the area. Yes, he'd been a major competitor of theirs. No, they'd not spoken to him directly for a couple of years. No, they certainly hadn't seen him yesterday. In fact, they'd not been anywhere yesterday. They'd spent the day together down here in Cosy Corner, and there'd been a continual flow of people in the café and the grocery store all day. When they finally closed, just before six in the evening, Celia had baked the new batch of cakes and biscuits for today, then they'd collapsed upstairs with fish and chips for supper before heading to bed and an early night.

Later, as the detectives were leaving, DCI Harolds paused and smiled at the couple.

"I think that's probably it for now," she said. "We'll need at least one of you to give evidence at the inquest, but we'll let you know about that when the date's fixed." She paused, then turned to Celia. "Just one last question, if I may. We're having some difficulty tracing Stanley Wentworth's family. Do you have any idea where they might be?" But Celia couldn't give them any information at all.

CHAPTER 17

"It's no good putting it off any longer, my lad. You're going to have to make contact." Rory talked to himself as he pulled up the sheet on his rumpled bed and glanced around at the rest of the room. Growing up in Coventry, his adoptive parents, Susan and Michael Black, had drummed into him he needed to be responsible for his own room and his own toys. There was an inspection every Friday night and if anything was out of place, they sent him to bed with no supper. It gave him a great sense of freedom that he no longer had to worry about such things. But even he knew the mess had got out of hand in the past few days. He vowed he'd tidy up when he got back tonight. Didn't want to risk an earful from the nosy old biddy who ran this B&B. He'd told her he didn't need the room done every day, and he always kept the key with him when he went out. But he suspected she had a spare one and could let herself in whenever she wanted to. Tonight. He'd sort it all out tonight.

He glanced around at the only space he could call his own at the moment. It wasn't much, although he'd seen far worse. The single bed pushed against the wall behind the door had faded patterned sheets which looked as if they'd been in use since the 1990s or longer. But they were clean, and they matched. There was a tatty carpet runner on the lino floor next to the bed and a matching piece in front of the tiny sink. An old wardrobe, probably bought from a junk shop, was the only other piece of furniture. There was no heater, and the radiators were ancient. At this time of year it was warm enough, but he certainly didn't want to be there once the weather started changing. And he'd had enough of sharing the bathroom and toilet along the landing with the rest of the guests.

"Yes, definitely time to get on with the plan. Time to find myself a forever home," he murmured as he shut the door, locked it, and pocketed the key.

Rory had been in Devon for nearly a week now. He'd ridden around, getting the lie of the land, and monitoring his target. He'd found out about the Village Store in the parade of shops on the new estate in Coombesford. The Chestnuts, it was called, although according to someone he met in the pub, the only chestnut trees around there had disappeared, chopped down when the developers moved in to build the estate ten years before.

He'd even gone into the post office a few times. But every time, the target of his observations had been busy serving, talking to other members of staff, or on the phone–either ordering stock for the grocery store or chatting to friends.

Up to now, all he had was a pocket full of stamps he wasn't ever going to use–he never wrote to anyone–and the memory of a couple of rather unpalatable sausage rolls. No, making contact in the shop wouldn't work at all.

But by hanging around, he'd also learned about the apartments above the retail units. He'd even nipped up the stairs once to have a look around while no-one was about. The place was being kept nice, judging by the plants outside the front door, and it looked big enough to have two bedrooms. Rory was feeling very hopeful about the whole thing.

He was determined to introduce himself and have that

chat today. With a bit of luck, he'd only have to return to the B&B once more, to collect his stuff. Of course, he'd paid up to the end of this week–old Mrs Nosy had insisted on that–but he didn't mind losing the money if he could get his feet under the table in Coombesford instead.

The traffic from Teignmouth was quite light. He took the road through Bishopsteignton and Newton Abbot. It was longer, but he'd only tried the back lanes over the Haldon Hills once and it had frightened him so much. His bike was quite wide and some places where he met vehicles coming the other way had been so narrow. And those local drivers didn't slow down, did they? He found himself stuck in the hedge once when he swerved out of the way of a huge Chelsea tractor full of excited kids, presumably being driven home from school. He supposed he'd get used to the country lanes once he'd been living here for a while, but for now, he was going to stick to the main roads.

Leaving the A38 at the Chudleigh turn-off, he drove through the small town and headed back into the countryside, reaching Coombesford within a couple of minutes. The car park of The Falls was full. Looked as if the pub was busy today. Maybe they'd go out for a drink later, to celebrate their reunion. Of course, he was skint until his next unemployment payment arrived, but he was sure that wouldn't be a problem. Just think of all the money saved on the expense of his upbringing. In his view, he had some funding due to him–about twenty-five years' worth!

Turning into The Chestnuts, he noticed it seemed busier than the previous times he'd been there. Then, there'd been no-one about, although he'd heard the occasional lawnmower or chainsaw in the back gardens. Now, there were groups of people standing on the street talking. And several residents seemed to have decided today was the day to weed their front gardens.

As he reached the end of Hill View and the parade of shops, the first thing he saw was a police car idling at the kerb outside the Village Store. One officer, a middle-aged man, was sitting in the passenger seat talking to someone on the radio. The other, a young woman, was standing in the doorway of the Village Store. What was going on? Had there been a robbery? Surely no-one would go to the trouble of knocking off a little rural place like this in broad daylight?

But at that moment, there was a movement from within the shop. A middle-aged redhead walked out carrying her handbag and her jacket. She turned and locked the door. Rory could see the sign on the inside said 'Closed'. The woman seemed to be crying. The policewoman put her arm around her shoulders and walked her across to the police car. She climbed into the back and sat in silence, wiping her eyes with a tissue. The police woman got into the driving seat and started the car. As they drove away, Rory heard a woman in the garden across the road talk to her next-door neighbour.

"Poor thing. It must be traumatic for her. She's gone to identify the body, you know. Anyway, nothing more to see here. Do you fancy a coffee?"

As the two women turned away to continue their gossip indoors, Rory started his bike and thoughtfully drove away. It looked as though he'd be spending a little while longer in the B&B, after all.

CHAPTER 18

DCI Andrea Harolds placed a photo face down on the coffee table and sat in silence, observing the woman on the sofa opposite her. Amelia Johnson was pressing her trembling lips together and unconsciously tearing at a tissue, scattering shreds of paper across her lap. She'd stopped crying by the time she'd arrived in the police car, although her eyes were red and puffy. Now she looked up and smiled weakly.

"I'm ready, DCI Harolds." Harolds turned over the photo and pushed it across the table. The other woman nodded once. "Yes. That's him. That's Stanley Wentworth." She pressed her hands to her mouth as tears ran down her cheeks. Harolds moved the box of tissues closer to Amelia. DS Smith poured a glass of water and placed it next to the tissues.

For a few moments, there was no sound in the room, then Amelia looked up, pushed her shoulders back and exhaled sharply. She looked straight at DCI Harolds.

"You need to find who did this terrible thing," she said. "What can I do to help, Detectives?"

"Well, if you're up to it, it would be useful to get some background information from you. How was Mr Wentworth viewed in the village? Did he have any enemies?

Anyone who might want to do him harm?"

Amelia was shaking her head even before the DCI had finished her questions.

"Oh no, I don't think it could be anyone local. They all loved Stanley, Mr Wentworth." Harolds was fairly certain that was a rather rosy-eyed view of the situation, but she kept that to herself for the moment as the other woman carried on speaking. "But there have been some strangers around lately, and he didn't seem at all pleased to see them."

"Strangers? Like who?"

"Well, there was a Mediterranean-looking man. Daniel something, Stanley called him." She bit her lip, then clicked her fingers. "Esposito! That was it. Daniel Esposito. Stanley told me they were old friends, but it didn't look friendly to me. It looked like they were arguing. And then Stanley sent me home early. He never does… did that. Later, he talked about owing Esposito a favour, and how it was going to cost him a lot of money. But he didn't go into details."

"And do you know where this Mr Esposito lives? Is he staying in the village?"

"No, I don't think so. But he drives a big silver 4x4. I grabbed a picture of it when he was in the Village Store. Not sure why. I just felt it might be important." She pulled her phone from her bag, swiped her fingers across the screen a few times, and turned it so DCI Harolds could see the picture. "There. That's the vehicle; and that's the registration number."

"Thank you, Ms Johnson. That's very helpful." DS Smith was taking rapid notes. "You mentioned strangers in the plural? Anyone else?"

"Well, there's that Maureen Walsh. Big blousy Irish woman, staying at The Falls." Amelia Johnson sniffed and twisted her mouth. "She reckons she's his wife. But according to Stanley, they split up some years back, and he thought they were divorced. He was happy enough when she first arrived, but when she talked about moving back in, that didn't please him at all. Maybe he turned her down, and she took her revenge."

"So, let me get this straight. There are two strangers from Mr Wentworth's past, both turning up unexpectedly, and neither was welcome. All seems a bit of a coincidence, doesn't it?"

Amelia shook her head.

"Not when you hear about the newspaper article. I entered us for a competition, you see, and we got shortlisted in the regional finals. Stanley was very uptight about it all. And now I can understand why." Her hand flew to her mouth. "Oh my God," she gasped. "It's my fault, isn't it? I wrote the article and sent it in. His past caught up with him. And now he's dead." She stared into space for a long moment, then returned her gaze to the two detectives. "I killed Stanley Wentworth, didn't I?"

CHAPTER 19

"I'm just popping over to The Falls, Roger," said Celia as Roger came in through the door from the backyard. "Annie's run short of a couple of things in the kitchen and they're not planning on going into Newton until next week." She held up a tub of flour and some jars of spices for Roger to see.

"That's not like Annie," he said. "She's normally so well organised." He paused and looked across the café at his wife. "I didn't hear the phone ring."

"It didn't. Young Suzy popped her head round the door on her way into school this morning."

"Okay, well, you carry on. I want to get this stocktaking done before the mid-morning rush begins. Take your phone and I'll text you if it gets busy."

As Celia crossed the village green heading for the old thatched gastropub, she smiled to herself. Roger's idea of a rush was two people waiting while he dealt with a third. Goodness knows how he'd cope if they had a place in Exeter or Newton Abbot. But that would never happen. The Cosy Corner business had been in her family since her grandparents' time and she certainly wouldn't want to work anywhere else.

When she reached The Falls, she headed around the side

of the building and pushed open the back door. She could hear movement from the kitchen, and headed towards the sound. Annie McLeod was standing in front of the large stove, stirring something in a pot. Her vivid pink hair was cut in a ragged urchin style. She looked over her shoulder as Celia tapped on the door and a huge grin split her face.

"Celia, how lovely to see you. How's things?" Then her expression changed, and she dropped the spoon and pulled the pan off the flames. "Oh goodness, I forgot. I'm sorry to hear about Stanley; we both are. It must have been terrible for you." She ran across the kitchen and held out her arms. "Come here, sweetie."

Celia felt tears prick her eyes briefly, and she pulled a little face.

"Thank you, Annie." She hugged the other woman tightly. It was good to wrap her arms around her friends once more without worrying. Sometimes a virtual hug just didn't cut it. "Yes, it was a shock, although I only saw the body from a distance. Roger wouldn't let me get too close." She paused, then went on. "But how did you know? I didn't think the police had made an official announcement yet."

"Village chatter," said Annie, grinning once more. "It never fails. Someone in the bar last night mentioned the body in Stover Country Park. Someone else said the Village Store up on the new estate was closed all day and there'd been police cars parked outside. Then someone else said they'd seen DCI Harolds sniffing around. And before long, the entire story was out there—and several other stories as well, to be honest."

"Yes, I get the picture," said Celia with a laugh. "Look, I can see you're busy, so I'll let you get back to the stove. Is Charlie around? I'd like a quick word."

"Sure. She's in the bar getting ready for the lunchtime opening." Annie stared at her friend, then blew her a kiss. "Glad to see you're okay. But if you need a chat, you know where I am." And with a little wave, she turned back to her cooking.

Celia carried on down the corridor and pushed open the door into the bar. Charlie Jones, in shorts and an Exeter Chiefs tee-shirt, was crouched down behind the counter, fiddling with the valve on one of the beer pumps. "Come on, you stupid thing, shift yourself," she muttered. Her long straight hair fell down her back in a ponytail, but her fringe flopped over her eyes. She pushed it back out of the way as if she was swatting a fly.

"Having trouble, Charlie?" asked Celia. Charlie jumped and looked over her shoulder.

"Celia, I didn't hear you come in. How are you this morning?"

Charlie and Annie were good friends with the Richardsons. Their two establishments were the only retail businesses in the village, if you didn't count the store on the new estate—and they didn't. Their friendship had strengthened during the investigation into Simon Mountjoy's murder three years ago. The café was where Charlie and Annie headed for a late lunch some afternoons. The pub was where Roger and Celia often ended the evening after a busy day behind their respective counters.

"I'm doing fine. Thanks for asking," Celia replied. Then she shook her head and pursed her lips. "Actually, that's not really true. Do you have a couple of minutes, Charlie? I'd like to pick your brains."

"Sure. There's plenty of time before we open. Come on outside and we'll get a bit of fresh air at the same time. Do you want a coffee or anything?"

"No, you're okay. I can't stay long. I told Roger I was just dropping off a few things you'd run out of. He'll be expecting me back soon. But yes, sitting outside would be lovely."

Once they'd sat down at an old wooden table in the beer garden behind the pub, Charlie looked at Celia with her head on one side.

"Right, then. What's the problem?"

Celia rubbed her hands over her face and stared across

at her friend, feeling those tears threatening once again. "It's Roger. He's been so quiet since yesterday and I can't help feeling there's something he's not telling me."

"Well, discovering a body is upsetting for anyone, Celia. Especially when it's someone you know. And even though Roger and Stanley didn't get on, it must have been terrible for him seeing the man dead like that."

"Didn't get on? That's an understatement," said Celia with a sad little smile. "But yes, I know you're right." She stared into the distance for a while, then shook her head. "Oh, I don't know, Charlie. Maybe it's nothing. But twice in the past week he's disappeared for an hour or so in the evenings. And when I asked where he'd been, he said 'nowhere'!"

"Celia, are you worried that Roger had something to do with Stanley's death? Because I really don't think there's anything for you to be concerned about. You know your husband's too soft to get involved in anything violent. He's just not that type. Whereas the same cannot be said about Mr Stanley Wentworth. We all know he had a very shady past. This is much more likely to be a duck from the old days that's finally come home to roost."

"Chicken, Charlie, not duck! If you're going to live in the countryside, and use rural sayings, you really should be able to sort one type of poultry from another!" Celia shook her head and her eyes sparkled with laughter. Townie Charlie was famous for her lack of wildlife knowledge. Then she became serious once more. "Yes, I know Roger's an old softie, Charlie. He would never deliberately do anything to harm even his worst enemy—and Stanley Wentworth certainly qualified for that role. But what if he's mixed up in something that's got out of hand?"

"What did the police say when they came to Cosy Corner last night?"

"You know about that, do you? Well, they were very nice and seemed satisfied with our answers, but you never know, do you, with those two? They're very good at playing their cards close to their chests."

"Celia," Charlie reached across the table and took hold of her friend's hand, "what would you like me to do?"

"I'm really not sure. But I thought, with your background, you might have some ideas."

"Look, why don't we have a chat with Rohan? Maybe he could do a bit of digging, find out what Roger's hiding. He was helping you out yesterday, wasn't he?"

"Yes, he was, and I would've said something to him then, but Roger was around all the time. Would you give him a ring for me, Charlie? I know he's not too busy at the moment."

"Yes, of course I will. Although the police will hopefully find something pretty quickly that'll sort this all out."

At that moment there was a loud clanging, like the sound of the school bell. Charlie looked around with a puzzled look on her face, but Celia pulled her mobile out of her pocket.

"That's me. Roger says there's a crowd of folks just arrived at the café. I need to get back there quickly." She stood and put her hand on Charlie's shoulder. "Thanks for the chat, Charlie. I feel a lot better. But if Rohan can do a bit of digging, that would be great." She walked across the beer garden, then stopped and turned back, holding out the packages she'd brought with her. "Oh, you'd better give these to Annie. I told Roger she'd run out of some stuff and that was my excuse for coming over here. I can't take them back with me."

"Okay, will do. What do we owe you?" But Celia shook her head.

"On the house, Charlie. Or maybe take it as a down payment on Rohan's fees. If he can help reassure me that my Roger has nothing to hide concerning Stanley's death, it will be well worth the money."

CHAPTER 20

While the yeast was rising in the warm milk on the edge of the Aga, Esther measured out the bread flour, salt and sugar into her largest bowl. It was not quite seven, and she had more than an hour before her father was due in for breakfast. There were going to be a couple of extra for lunch today, and she wanted to make sure she had enough fresh bread to go with the huge pan of vegetable broth she'd made yesterday.

Esther had been baking bread almost daily for years and could follow the process in her sleep. Which was just as well, since she knew she wasn't really concentrating this morning. Mixing the wet and dry ingredients together, she set the dough hook running and switched on the kettle for her first mug of tea. As she inhaled the aroma from her Earl Grey and Rose Sencha mix, she thought back to the conversation she'd had with her father last night.

News of Stanley Wentworth's death had reached her via Celia Richardson, when she'd called to collect her latest order of eggs. Celia had been quieter than usual and was obviously still suffering from shock.

"To be honest, Esther, I'm hiding out up here. The café's been packed all morning. And everyone wants to hear our story again. It was getting on my nerves! So I just walked out and left Roger to it."

"Oh dear. Poor Roger."

Celia shrugged and smiled a guilty little smile.

"He'll be fine. Loves being the centre of attention, he does. And I'll make it up to him later. I'm baking his favourite for supper—"

"Lasagne with loads of garlic!" chimed in Esther. Roger was well known for his love of Italian food, especially if it involved lots of creamy sauces and cheese.

Having heard the facts from Celia, rather than the wild rumours flying around on Facebook, Esther could give her father a pretty accurate account that evening.

"And the police think someone poisoned him. They definitely suspect foul play," she concluded.

"Hmm. Couldn't have happened to a nicer chap," was her father's surprising response.

"Dad, that's a terrible thing to say," she gasped. "It's not like you to speak ill of people."

Her father pulled a face.

"Yes, I know it sounds harsh. But Stanley Wentworth has been nothing but trouble ever since he first arrived in the village all those years ago. He split up Celia from Roger before dumping her and running away. And since Simon Mountjoy brought him back and installed him in the Village Store, he's done his level best to spoil the business at Cosy Corner. Yes, I reckon Coombesford will be a better place without him."

And opening the local newspaper, he'd turned to the farming pages and settled down to read. Neither of them mentioned Stanley Wentworth again. But now, as she turned the dough out onto a board and began kneading it, Esther wondered just why her father felt so unsympathetic towards the murdered man.

CHAPTER 21

"Welcome to the mean streets of Teignmouth, my friend. It's good to see you on my territory for a change." Rohan Banerjee unzipped his jacket and executed a couple of lunges before leaning back on the railing next to Charlie. The view across The Den was of faded Victorian buildings in the background, and a children's play park in the foreground. They'd just jogged at a fairly rapid rate along the length of the esplanade and back. It impressed Charlie that her old friend seemed not to be even slightly out of breath. She'd needed to bend over, resting her hands on her knees, desperately trying to recover. It was several minutes before she'd been able to straighten up and join him in his contemplation of the seaside town.

"Boy, but I'm out of condition," she wheezed. "There was a time when I could've done three times that distance without breaking a sweat…"

"Time and age catch up with all of us," said Rohan, "or so I've been told. I'll let you know when I get there!" He laughed and dodged away as Charlie swatted at his arm. "But seriously, Charlie, it's only a matter of practice. I've been doing this every morning since I moved down here. It's beautiful when the sun shines and magnificent when it's stormy. And quiet at this time of the morning. You're welcome to join me any time you like."

Charlie smiled and patted him on the back.

"Yes, I know and maybe I'll take you up on the offer occasionally, but there's always so much to do in the mornings, what with sorting breakfast for the guests and getting Suzy ready for school. Annie and I rarely have time to breathe, let alone think about going out for a run."

"You could always bring them with you. During the holidays or at weekends, at least."

"Yeah, right." Charlie gave a snort of derision. Annie had never been one for running. She got her exercise in the pool. And the idea of their eleven-year-old daughter coming out and running in the early morning light with her mothers was just laughable. She looked at her watch. It was fast approaching seven. "Look, I'm going to have to go in a few minutes, I'm afraid, but I wanted to consult you professionally first."

"So it wasn't just the lure of fresh air and running with me that brought you down here," said Rohan with a smile. He turned and stared out across the open water. "I thought you sounded mysterious on the phone last night. What can I do for you, then?"

Rohan Banerjee had been a serving police officer, with a talent for amateur dramatics and a growing reputation for undercover work in his native Manchester, before an unfortunate occurrence during the trial of a drug-dealing gang leader had blown his cover and made life a bit too hot to handle. He'd resigned from the force and become a private investigator, moving initially to London. During a trip to Devon to help Charlie investigate Simon Mountjoy's murder, he'd fallen in love with the southwest and had moved down not long afterwards, just before the world went into lockdown. Like many people, he'd found the pandemic a tough time to start a business, but he'd held on, and Charlie knew things were improving. At the moment, he still worked occasional shifts at The Falls and Cosy Corner to help pay the rent on the small bedsit from which he ran his personal and professional lives, but he'd told his friends at both establishments they should not rely on him long-term.

"I had a visit from Celia yesterday morning."

"Poor Celia. What a terrible thing, finding someone dead like that. And then to realise it was someone she knew. How's she holding up? She was pretty distraught when they got back Wednesday morning."

"Actually, she seems to be doing pretty well. She's made of stern stuff, our Celia. And she got over Stanley Wentworth a long time ago. Even if Roger didn't completely believe her."

"What's the problem, then?"

"She's worried about Roger." Charlie turned her back on the town and stared out at sea. In the distance, a couple of hardy early morning swimmers were racing between the pier and the end of the esplanade, but otherwise, the view was empty. "They both appear to have satisfied the police they had nothing to do with Stanley's murder." Rohan's head swivelled round, and he looked askance at Charlie. "Yes, it was murder. Sorry, I thought you knew."

"No, I didn't. When I left them on Wednesday afternoon, they were talking about him having some sort of heart attack or similar. So it wasn't natural causes? How did he die?"

"Poison, they think. Our old friends DCI Harolds and DS Smith went round to Cosy Corner that evening."

Rohan gave a huge smile and clapped his hands.

"Pepper Pig and her salty sidekick are on the case, are they? Definitely murder then. They don't leave the environs of the big city for anything less." He rubbed his hands together. "And you want me to see if I can beat them to it, do you?"

"Not necessarily. But Celia tells me Roger has been acting a bit strangely lately."

"No change there," said the young man, but Charlie didn't need to hear the affection in his friend's voice to know he was joking. The couple from Cosy Corner treated Rohan almost like a son, and she knew Rohan, separated from his own large family by hundreds of miles, reciprocated the feeling.

"Apparently he's gone missing in the evenings a couple of times lately," Charlie went on, "and when Celia challenged him on it, he hasn't had a reasonable explanation for her. She's worried he's got himself mixed up in something and it might have got out of hand."

"You want me to see if I can find out what he's involved in? That should be easy enough," said Rohan. "I'm doing another shift for them tomorrow. Celia's having a couple of days away at some health spa." Charlie raised her eyebrows, and Rohan sniggered. "Yes, I know it doesn't sound like the good Celia's bag, but it was a birthday present from Olga. Apparently, the pair of them are going to be away for the entire weekend. Mind you, she's doing all the baking before she goes, so she'll need the rest by the time she gets there. Roger asked me to cover for her. And I've got nothing on the books at the moment, apart from a straightforward surveillance job that I'll have tied up by early next week. I was happy to say yes." He paused. "And to be honest, I could do with the money. If you need me to do any shifts at The Falls while I'm up your way, just shout."

"Okay, will do. And if you want a bed for the night, to save driving back over the hills, just let me know. But a day in Cosy Corner will be perfect. You can keep an eye on Roger and maybe get him to talk about what's going on." Charlie bent and retied the shoelace on her trainer that had come loose during their run. Then she straightened up and pulled her car keys out of her running belt. "Now, I really must be going. It's Mrs Wilson's funeral today and we're holding the wake at The Falls afterwards."

"Yes, I know," said Rohan, pushing himself away from the railings. "I'm coming over for that. Have to support Pauline, don't we? Right, I'll walk you back to the car. Then I might just take a run up to East Cliff park. The flowerbeds are looking wonderful and it looks like it's going to be far too nice a day to go back to the flat."

As the friends strolled back along the esplanade, Charlie pondered the murder of Stanley Wentworth once more.

"You know, Rohan, maybe it's not such a bad idea for you to look into Stanley Wentworth's murder, too. I know you were only joking about stealing a march on the Exeter duo, but from what Celia and Roger have said occasionally, he had a pretty shady past and spent some of it in prison. Maybe his death has nothing to do with Coombesford or anyone in the village. Maybe he upset someone in the past and they've finally caught up with him. There's been more than one stranger to the village looking for him recently, since that newspaper article appeared." She stopped, and Rohan stopped with her. "Yes, do that. See what you can find out from your contacts about Stanley Wentworth's past." She put her hand on his arm. "And I insist on this being a paid gig." She held up her hand to silence him as he opened his mouth, apparently to argue. "Yes, I know you're being paid to work with Roger, and anything you can find out about him will be as a favour to Celia, but you're running a business here. And favours are no good when it comes time to pay the rent. If you're doing additional work for me on Stanley Wentworth's background, then you must charge me for it."

Charlie watched her friend's eyes well momentarily with tears and he swallowed hard before nodding his thanks. She wondered just how difficult Rohan was finding it at the moment. She resolved to talk to Annie about whether there was anything more they could do to help without offending the proud young man who was trying hard to succeed in his new life here in Devon. For now, she opened her arms wide.

"Big hug, my friend. Thanks for the run. And for showing me just how out of condition I am. Let's do it again soon. Maybe we'll run around the lanes while you are in the village next week?" Blowing him a kiss, she climbed into her elderly but spotless Fiat and headed for the Haldon Hills and another busy day in Coombesford.

CHAPTER 22

"Are you okay in here for a while, Charlie? I need to get back to the kitchen and start laying out the meat platters."

Charlie stood up from where she'd been checking the supply of mixers in the cool cabinet under the bar and looked across at her partner. She told herself once again just how lucky she was to be living in such a wonderful part of the world with this woman.

"Yes, I'm fine. You carry on. There's not much else to do now. I've just got to finish topping up this lot." She glanced up at the big backwards clock hanging at the end of the room, one fixture she and Annie took on when they bought The Falls just under four years ago. "We'll need to get changed pretty soon, though. Are you going to be ready in time?"

"Yes, another half hour should do it. The funeral's not until midday; and at least we only have to walk across the road to the church. But we need to get there a bit early if we can. I reckon it'll be full."

"Good point. And we'd better sit at the back. We can slip out quickly once the service is over."

The entire village was likely to turn out for Mrs Winifred Wilson's funeral. Some because they were contemporaries of the woman and her late husband; others because they were friends of her unmarried daughter and, in recent years, carer Pauline. The Wilson women had lived in a small two-bedroomed house on The Chestnuts estate for the past few years, having bought it from new when their previous old cottage with a large garden became too much for Mrs Wilson to manage. Pauline readily admitted she didn't have green fingers or an interest in gardening. The new property with just a tiny paved patch front and back was much more to her liking.

Mrs Wilson was in her late seventies at the time of her death and had been a widow for over twenty-five years, after a tragic accident with a tractor during a thunderstorm took the life of her husband. She'd been slipping into dementia since before Charlie and Annie moved to Devon, and they'd never known the independent, feisty woman everyone told them she'd once been. But they realised she would have had to be strong to bring up a child on her own under those circumstances. And they'd got to know Pauline over the past three years, particularly since Charlie saved her life one dramatic night. They knew she had very mixed feelings about her mother's death. It was devastating to lose her at a relatively early age. But to pass away peacefully in her sleep from a heart attack was infinitely preferable to the ongoing deterioration and gradual loss from dementia. Pauline had told them she knew, once she got over the immediate grief, she'd be very grateful for the way her mother's life ended.

It was twenty minutes later, as Charlie was about to head back over to the Folly, their little house behind the beer garden, that the outside door into the bar suddenly flew open.

"I'm afraid we're closed at the moment, for a private function," Charlie began, but stopped when she saw the tall, plump woman with short blonde hair standing in the doorway. Her outfit of black dress, black stockings and flat black shoes drained all the colour from her skin. She had dark rings around her eyes and there was a look of abject horror on her face. Charlie rushed over to the door and pulled the woman into the room.

"Pauline, sweetie, are you okay?" She knew that was a pretty dumb question. How could she be okay on the day of her mother's funeral? But when they'd seen Pauline Wilson the previous evening, to confirm the numbers for the wake, she'd looked composed and dignified, if sad. Now she was anything but.

"Charlie, it's horrible. We can't bury her! The police say we have to wait!" And with a howl, she threw herself into Charlie's arms and cried. Annie, hearing the commotion, came rushing in from the kitchen. For the next few minutes, there was nothing but loud sobs from Pauline. Charlie looked at Annie over the distraught woman's shoulder and raised her eyebrows.

Eventually, the storm subsided. Pauline disengaged herself from Charlie's arms and took the tissues Annie held out to her.

"I'm sorry," she said, "but it's such a bombshell. I don't know what to do. All those people! What are we going to tell them?"

Annie took Pauline by the arm and steered her towards a chair.

"Okay, Pauline, take a deep breath and start from the beginning."

Pauline stared at her friends for a long moment in silence, then shook her head and began speaking.

"I was just getting ready when I had a call from the undertaker. I thought he was ringing to tell me all the flowers had arrived safely–everyone has been so generous, there's going to be a tremendous display around the coffin." She paused. "At least there was going to be. But now, I'm not sure whether there's any point in carrying on with the service." She stopped again. "The vicar! I wonder if anyone's told him yet? Well, I guess he'll know something's up as soon as he looks out of his bedroom window, seeing as how there are police crawling all over his graveyard."

Charlie looked at Annie and asked a question with her

eyes. Annie's response was to shake her head. Pauline started talking again.

"I suppose we can go ahead with the service, then come back here for the wake. But it'll seem really strange, knowing Mum's on her way back to the funeral parlour instead of being reunited with Dad as we expected."

Finally, Charlie's patience ran out.

"Pauline Wilson, will you please tell us what is going on? You're not making any sense at all. Why would the service not go ahead? And why on earth would your mother be going back to the funeral parlour?"

"Because the police say we can't bury Mum in the family grave until they finish their investigation."

"Investigation? What investigation?"

"Into the body in the grave, of course. Didn't I say? When they opened the grave, they found another body in there."

Annie looked as confused as Charlie was feeling at that moment.

"But, Pauline love, it's your family grave. Your father has been in there for a long time. Why is the sight of a body in there causing so much upset?"

Pauline shook her head vigorously.

"No, Annie, they found a second body in there. When they opened the grave, there was a decomposed body lying down the side of the coffin. They called the police and now there's a tent over the site, police everywhere, and I've been told they don't know how long it'll be before we can lay Mum to rest." Throughout this speech, which all came out in a bit of a rush, Pauline's voice had been getting higher and higher. By the end, it was more of a wail than anything else.

Charlie and Annie stared at each other. Then Charlie decided it was time to take charge.

"Annie, will you pop over to the vicarage and check whether the reverend knows about the discovery? And see what his view is about going ahead with the service? Pauline, you and I will phone the funeral director and talk it through with him. Once we know what the options are, you can decide what you want to do. As you said, there's a lot of people due here in an hour and a half; and I assume some of them are coming from outside Coombesford?" Pauline nodded. "Well, we've got lunch all ready, so no-one needs to go away hungry. We could hold the service and the wake today as planned and then, once the police have finished their investigation and released the grave, maybe you could have a quiet committal service with just a few close friends." She held out her hand and pulled their friend to her feet. "But whatever you decide to do, your mother would approve. You know she trusted your judgment."

Pauline smiled a watery smile.

"Yes, you're right, Charlie." She paused and gave a little giggle. "And she's hardly able to complain, now is she?" Pauline put her hand over her mouth and looked shocked at her irreverent comment, but the giggles continued and it was a while before Charlie could get her calmed down enough to make the phone call to the funeral director.

In the end, everyone agreed to go with Charlie's suggestion. The service was beautiful. The flowers were, as Pauline had predicted, magnificent. And the array of food put on by Charlie and Annie at the wake—at no cost to Pauline, it was their contribution to the day—was such that no-one in Coombesford needed to cook dinner that evening.

Like most wakes, there were a few tears, but a lot of laughter and reminiscences. But also, there was another topic of conversation, one that no-one had expected to be discussing that lunchtime. Everyone wanted to know who was the unexpected visitor to the Wilsons' family plot. Was it a man or a woman? How long had they been there, and why?

CHAPTER 23

"Esther, are you there? It's Annie. Can I come in?"

"Sure, Annie, come on in. I'm in the kitchen." The voice was clear and bright. Annie guessed it was one of Esther Steele's good days.

She walked down the passageway into what had become one of her favourite rooms in the whole of Coombesford village. Esther, her straight white blonde hair held back from her face with an old-fashioned Alice band, was standing at the vast oak table, the centrepiece of the kitchen. The centrepiece, in fact, of the whole farmhouse, Annie suspected. She was rolling pastry and, as she pushed her fringe out of her eyes with the back of her hand, she left a smudge of flour on her nose. Her smile was huge, welcoming, and genuine. Annie always felt at home when she came to visit this place and especially this woman.

"Annie, how wonderful to see you. Give me a minute to get these in the oven and I'll put the kettle on."

"No hurry, Esther. It's been hectic over the past couple of days. I'm happy just to sit and watch you create for a few minutes."

Her host's face clouded over and she sighed.

"Yes, one of the farmhands told me. Poor Pauline. She must be frantic, waiting to hear what's going to happen."

"She's holding up okay, actually. The service and the wake went as well as she could have hoped; and she's planning a very simple committal service when the police finally release the site."

"That's good to hear. I haven't seen her for ages, since she started caring for her mum, in fact. But we used to be quite close. We were at primary school together, you know. And after the accident, she used to come and visit me here at the farm." Esther walked across to the Aga and popped a tray of delicate apple tarts in the oven. "There, they won't take long and we can have one with our tea in a little while." She wiped her hands on a tea towel and began filling the kettle.

While the kettle gently hissed on the top of the Aga, Esther took one of the large rocking chairs beside the open fireplace and gestured for Annie to take the other. The chairs were a riot of colour with hand-stitched patchwork cushions, into which the two women sank with sighs of delight. At this time of year the fire was never lit, and the cradle was full, not with burning logs, but with piles of sweet-smelling pine cones. A huge vase of dahlias and chrysanths stood on the hearth.

"Okay, Annie, what brings you here this morning?" asked Esther. "Not that you need a reason to stop by, my friend, but I know how busy you usually are in the mornings."

"I wanted to see how you were getting on with Suzy's picture. And I needed some more eggs, so I thought I'd pop in rather than just picking up the phone."

"Well, the picture's coming along nicely. I should have something to show you early next week. And yes, we've got loads of eggs. They're in the cabinet in the mud room. You can help yourself on your way out."

The two women continued chatting until the kitchen timer pinged and Esther rose to make the tea and pull the baked pies from the oven. The aroma was enticing, a mixture of pastry, stewed apple, and cinnamon. Annie felt her mouth water in anticipation. Within minutes Esther was back in her seat, and the two women were blowing on their pies, eager to get started but aware of the dangers of burning apple juice.

For the next few minutes there was no further talk, just appreciative murmurs from both women. Annie had two pies, telling herself she would go for an extra-long swim later on to burn off the additional calories.

As they finished, the front doorbell rang.

"I wonder who that can be," said Esther, rising to her feet. "No-one from around here ever comes to the front door. They always come around to the back like you did." She left the kitchen door open as she walked into the hall. Annie heard a murmur of voices and then Esther returned to the kitchen, followed by DCI Harolds and DS Smith. The two nodded and smiled at Annie, then took the seats offered to them by Esther.

"They're looking for Dad," she told Annie, "but he's gone up to North Devon to look at some cattle he's thinking of buying. I'm not expecting him back until late tonight. And he's switched his phone off."

"I should go," said Annie, wiping her mouth and fingers on an embroidered napkin from the tea tray. But the DCI held out an arm and stopped her.

"Maybe you could hang on for a few moments, Annie. We've got some news for Ms Steele and she might appreciate your company."

Annie and Esther looked at each other in alarm. Annie remained seated, and Esther sat down in her chair with a thud. The DCI continued.

"Ms Steele, there's no easy way for me to say this. But we've identified the body in the Wilsons' grave." She swallowed hard. Annie had never seen Andrea Harolds look nervous before. "I'm sorry to have to tell you it's Mrs June Steele. It looks like she didn't run away as you and your father believed, but she was killed and her body was hidden in Mr Wilson's grave twenty-six years ago." The DCI reached over and took Esther's hands in hers. "Ms Steele, Esther, we've found your mother."

CHAPTER 24

Annie retraced her steps to the back door of Fosters Farm the following day as soon as she'd finished serving breakfast at The Falls. There were no cars in the farmyard, and she guessed Tommy Steele had gone into Exeter to talk to the police.

After DCI Harolds had made her announcement the previous morning, Annie had watched as Esther seemed slowly shut down. There had been no tears; just a long, shocked silence that persisted while DS Smith refreshed the teapot and delivered mugs all round. It continued after the two detectives had departed for Exeter, leaving a message for Esther's father to get in touch as soon as he arrived back from North Devon. And it was still going on when the farmer got home. Annie had tried ringing him, but his mobile had remained turned off. She therefore found herself in the unenviable position of having to give him the news of the discovery of his wife's body.

Farmer Steele had been more controlled than his daughter, but it was obvious to Annie that the news came as a blow to him too. When they'd first come to Coombesford, she and Charlie had heard rumours about this man. How he was rude and distant. But once Annie's friendship with Esther had developed, she'd realised he was

93

shy rather than anything else, and not used to dealing with people, as he spent much of his time on his own or with the farmhands, tending his fields or herding his animals from one part of the farm to another. But more than anything else, what made Annie warm towards this man was his absolute devotion to his daughter, a damaged young woman who rarely left the house.

Once the initial shock of Annie's announcement had worn off, Tommy politely but firmly suggested it was time for her to return The Falls and leave him to look after Esther. He had, however, been grateful when she'd offered to return the following day to keep Esther company while he headed into Exeter to "sort out this mess."

Now, Annie tapped on the door and, hearing a soft call from inside, pushed her way through the mud room filled with assorted boots and pegs containing raincoats and other clothing necessary for anyone used to working outside all year round in Devon's weather. In the kitchen, she found Esther sitting in the rocking chair where she'd left her the evening before.

In fact, at first Annie wondered if her friend had spent the entire night there. But gradually, she noticed details that told her this wasn't the case.

Esther looked pale, but she had tied her hair back in a ponytail. She was wearing different clothes from the day before. The kitchen was as tidy as ever. On the table was a tray with mugs, a milk jug and a plate of home-made ginger biscuits. There was a lingering smell of baking in the air. Esther's old collie dog, Frisk, was lying on the floor at her feet. He raised his head to watch Annie enter the room, but apparently recognising she was no threat to his mistress, he thumped his tail twice on the floor and returned to his former position, with nose pressed against Esther's shoe and eyes trained on her face.

"Good morning, Annie." Esther's voice was quieter than normal, but fully under control. "Thank you for coming over so early. Dad's gone to Exeter. And I'm really glad of the company." She reached down and stroked Frisk's nose. "We both are, really. But I know how busy you guys can get at The Falls towards lunchtime, so if you need to go…"

"Don't be silly," replied Annie. "I'm happy to be here. Charlie's roped Rohan Banerjee in for a couple of days. I'm free for as long as you need me." She paused, biting her lip, then went on, "And Suzy would like to pop in this afternoon, if you're up to it."

"That would be wonderful. Although I'll need to put my sketchbook away before she arrives." She gestured to the large pad on the table. "I was up even earlier than usual this morning, and after I'd done the day's baking, I experimented with a few more ideas for her birthday present." Annie moved towards the table, but Esther shook her head. "No, don't look at it yet. I want to do more work before I'm ready to show you my ideas."

Esther gestured to the other rocking chair and Annie sank gratefully into the soft cushions.

"I must admit, I'm surprised to hear you've been baking this morning," she said. Esther smiled back at her.

"Well, we all have to eat, Annie, whatever else is going on. And the farm hands will expect their lunch as usual around midday." She grinned and whispered conspiratorially, "But I must admit to cheating today. I used the bread maker to make today's loaves. And I pulled the cookie dough out of the freezer. There wasn't much to do from scratch."

When the kettle had boiled and the two women had their mugs of tea to hand, Esther suggested they take them out into the garden. "It's such a beautiful day. And to be honest, I'm finding it claustrophobic indoors at the moment." She looked at Annie with a wicked grin. "And yes, I realise that's not a sentence you'd ever expect me to utter. But ironically, right now, it's true. Here," thrusting her mug at Annie, "you carry these and I'll bring the tray."

As they sat at a table under a pergola covered with roses

and honeysuckle, Annie stared around her in awe, as she had the first time she'd come out here. She'd learned later she was one of the very few people with whom Esther shared her outside haven. Close to the house there was a small paved area, with weathered bricks underfoot and enormous tubs bursting with colour: dahlias, geraniums and roses, lots of roses. But just outside the seated area, the planting changed. There was an octagonal herb garden, divided into eight by lines of pearly white stones. Each section was bursting to the seams with different varieties of the same plants: Annie recognised mint, parsley and sage, but wasn't sure about the rest. She knew Esther used these aromatic plants extensively in her cooking.

Past the herb garden were rows of runner beans, peas, and what Annie had been told were potato plants. To one side was a greenhouse stuffed full of overflowing pots. From her seat Annie could see the bright red of ripe tomatoes, and the yellows and oranges of sweet peppers, plus cucumbers and aubergines. And on the other side were a couple of apple trees. A high fence surrounded the entire plot, shutting out the view and making this a safe, enclosed space. The only outside space, Esther had told her, where she felt comfortable.

CHAPTER 25

"I was ten when my mother disappeared. But of course I knew nothing about it. I was still in the coma at that point." Esther rarely talked about the past, but today, it felt like the right thing to do. And it felt as if Annie was the right person to hear the story. "In fact, I remember nothing for six months after that day on Chudleigh Rocks.

"I'd run away from school, you see. Such a silly thing. We'd had a class vote to choose who would be May Queen that year. We'd been learning the steps for the maypole dancing– it was our turn to put on the show that year–and I was frankly rubbish! I kept getting my steps in the wrong order, turning the wrong way, bumping into people. I even caused a tangle one day that took us twenty minutes to undo. I knew I had to get out of it. And the obvious thing to do was to win the vote. The May Queen didn't take part in the dancing, you see. She sat on her throne and enjoyed the entertainment. Sitting still and looking regal; I was sure I could do that with no problem.

"But when they announced the result, I'd lost out by just one vote. I was so upset, I just walked out without talking to anyone." She stopped and shook her head. "And the real irony was that the staff were just as keen to keep me out of the dancing as I was. I only learned years later when one of my old school teachers came to visit, that they were planning to appoint an attendant for the May Queen, who could hold the Queen's train as she walked and then sit on a smaller chair next to the throne during the dancing.

"I was supposed to be going for a walk with Mum that afternoon, but she was late. And I didn't want to hang around, so I went on my own. I walked for miles—or so it seemed to a ten-year-old—and I found myself at the kissing gate in Rock Road, leading up onto Chudleigh Rocks. And something seemed to draw me on. The weather was beautiful, and the path was dry, so I climbed up the steep hill. When I got to the top, I found myself a little nook against the boulders and sat down to enjoy the view and watch the flowers grow." She paused and winked at Annie. "I was a really precocious child. But after a while I fell asleep. And when I woke up, the world had changed."

"How long were you asleep, then?"

"I really don't know. But it was early April, and the weather was changeable. It might only have been a few minutes; or it could have been several hours. It was the cold that woke me. The sunshine had disappeared. There was a stiff breeze blowing. Huge black clouds were rolling across the meadow towards me. And then it rained." She rubbed her arms and shuddered. "I can still feel it starting, even now. Initially, there were only a few drops; I could feel them as individual splashes landing on my skin. But then the heavens opened, and it was just like a sheet of water."

"Must have been terrifying." Esther's description was so vivid, Annie appeared to feel the cold and wet herself, shuddering, even in the sunny garden many years later.

"It was, Annie, it certainly was. I knew I had to get out of there. There was no shelter at all. I didn't have a raincoat. And to make it worse, I couldn't work out how to get down."

"But the path up the side of the hill? That's how you came up, wasn't it?"

"Yes, it was, but that path was notoriously dangerous

when it was wet, really slippery. Someone had fallen off there the previous year and we knew we shouldn't use it unless it was bone dry. Besides which, it ran through the woods and what had seemed perfectly harmless when the sun was shining down through the branches, had suddenly become a dark and menacing hole in the ground." Esther turned to Annie. "Have you ever been up there?" she asked. Annie shook her head.

"Well, the top of Chudleigh rocks is a plateau. To the north is the path through the wood. To the east and the south there's a sheer cliff looking down over the fields below. And to the west, there's the climbing wall."

"What, a man-made one, like they have in the gyms?"

"No, a natural one. The cliff face is much more rugged on that side, which is why many climbers use it for practice." She paused. "I decided that was the only way down for me."

"But you were a ten-year-old girl with no equipment and presumably no experience. How on earth did you think you were going to manage that climb?"

"Children are much more fearless than adults," Esther said, with a smile, "if lacking in logic sometimes. I was too scared to go back into the woods and risk the wet slippery path, but I didn't think twice about lowering myself over the edge of the cliff and climbing down." She paused, bit her lip as she felt her mouth tremble. As she continued, Esther's voice was quieter. "Of course, you know what happened next. And that was pretty much all I remember until I woke from the coma six months later. By which time my mother had disappeared. And it's been just Dad and me ever since."

"What happened when you finally came round? Were you still in hospital by then?"

"No, Dad brought me home to look after me. The doctors suggested I might never recover. But one day, I just woke up! I was weak, disorientated, and highly distressed. But physically, there was nothing wrong with me."

"That's amazing, isn't it? No ill effects at all?"

"I said there were no physical effects. I spent a while

recuperating and getting some strength back into my legs, but I was desperate to get back outside and see the animals again. Finally, Dad agreed I could go for a short walk. I wanted to do it by myself. He sat on the bench outside the front door and I headed off across the farmyard on my own." She stopped talking. Telling her story was proving to be more difficult than she'd expected. But after a few minutes, she sighed and shook her head. "I only made it as far as the gate into the top field. I felt a great weight pressing down on me. The sky seemed huge, the fields went on forever, and I was just a tiny insignificant speck. I screamed, turned and ran straight back to the house and didn't put my nose outside for the next eighteen months."

"Oh, Esther, I'm sorry," said Annie. "What was it? The stress of what you'd been through?"

Esther nodded.

"Yes. Dad got a top specialist to come and see me here at the farm. Goodness knows how he managed it. But he did. And the specialist diagnosed it as anxiety and panic attacks brought on by the shock of the accident, and possibly by the loss of my mother as well."

"And it's still with you, even today."

Esther nodded.

"This garden is as far as I can ever go on my own. I've only been off the property once or twice each year since, and always with Dad to look after me."

She stopped and looked around at their surroundings. "When I turned thirteen, Dad told me he had a surprise for me. This place here, where we're sitting, used to be a bit of scrub land between the farmhouse and the barns. He'd had it tidied up and flowerbeds put in. And this pergola. And because of the high fencing, it felt like I was still inside. For the first few days, I only came out when Dad was around, but gradually I got braver and finally, I was spending more time out here than I was in the house.

"The next year, Dad added a bit more space, and we planted those raspberry canes over there. Then the year after, he had the greenhouse built and the herb bed laid. Gradually, he's developed this wonderful area for me. And I found I'd inherited his green fingers and started growing all these vegetables. For most of the year, we're self-sufficient."

The two women sat quietly for several moments. Esther realised there were tears pouring down her cheeks. Annie turned towards her and took her hand.

"Talking about the past must be really difficult, now they've found your mother, Esther?"

But Esther shook her head.

"No, it's not that. Yes, it was an eye-opener yesterday. Apparently, Mum blamed herself for my accident, missing our meeting at the school gate. When she disappeared a month later, there was no note, and she took nothing with her. Everyone always assumed she couldn't cope with my illness." She paused. "But now we find out she's been right here in the village all this time.

"For the last couple of years of her life, Mum suffered from terrible migraines. She spent more time in bed than she did running the house or looking after me. It was always Dad and me against the world, right from when I was seven or eight. And that's what scares me, Annie. In a case like this – a case of murder – it's always the closest people who fall under suspicion; often with justification." Esther felt sweat breaking out on her forehead and struggled to control her breathing. "I couldn't bear it, Annie, if the police took Dad away. I know he had nothing to do with Mum's death, he's just not like that. But it's so long ago. It's going to be impossible to find evidence. What if they try to pin it on him? What are we going to do, Annie?"

Up above, a cloud floated in front of the sun and chilly shadows reached down into the little garden. With a sob, Esther jumped up and ran back into the house, leaving Annie sitting alone under the pergola.

CHAPTER 26

"I guess it's home from home for you, Charlie, meeting in a pub like this?" said Rohan as he stretched his legs out in front of him and linked his fingers together behind the back of his head.

"Always good to check out the opposition once in a while," replied Charlie, taking a long swig from her pint of lime juice and soda. "Mind you," she went on, "I have to admit that even The Falls can't compete with this place in terms of view."

The pair had met up in the car park at the top of the steep hill rising away from the village of Shaldon and had strolled down to the large yellow, black and white building clinging to the side of the cliff. Named for the massive red sandstone headland on which it was located, The Ness was a nineteenth-century country house rejuvenated as a restaurant with rooms, popular with holidaymakers and locals alike. Mid-afternoon it was quiet, and Rohan had steered them through the bar area crowded with tables, and out onto the terrace, which they had to themselves.

The sky, cloudless and impossibly blue, reflected in the smooth flat water below. Black-headed gulls wheeled and shrieked in front of them, and although the distant shores of Shaldon and Teignmouth were both crowded with holidaymakers, this was the only sound they could hear.

"It is lovely here," Charlie went on. "Annie and I came down for a drink a while back. That disastrous time we left you in charge—"

"Look, Charlie, I've already explained. And it really wasn't my fault, you know. If I'd known they were going to let that goat run wild, I'd never have let them park their trailer outside The Falls."

Charlie patted his arm and grinned at him.

"It's okay, mate. I'm only teasing you." She paused and raised her eyebrows, "And I think Annie's more or less forgiven you for having to redo that one flowerbed completely." She took another gulp from her glass and then sat up straight, hands on knees. "Right then, let's hear what you've got to say. I've not got too long. I'll need to be back by four-thirty to help Annie open up."

Rohan pulled a notebook out of his backpack and flipped through until he found the right page.

"Well, I've managed to trace the history of Mr Stanley Adam Wentworth. Although it wasn't easy. He was one of those folks with several names. He was born Stanley Adams, in Coventry. His family moved around quite a lot. It looks like his father got into trouble more than once and they had to up sticks and move on before they got caught. They were just one step ahead of the law much of the time.

"Stanley seems to have been a bit of a chip off the old block. But whereas his father was just a petty criminal who never paid rent if he could help it, Stanley moved up a league or two. By the time he was nineteen, he was number two in a gang in the back streets of Birmingham. They were into drugs, prostitution, extortion, all sorts of things. Stanley rarely got his own hands dirty, but got himself a reputation as the Mr Fixit who always knew where to find a gun for hire, a very special woman, or the latest batch of crack cocaine coming in from Latin America.

"Then one night, he got too close to the action himself. A woman died following a shooting at a party that got out of hand and although there was nothing to prove our man pulled the trigger, he was definitely there and probably supplied the weapon. The police issued a warrant for his arrest. Except Stanley had enough experience of that sort of situation to know it was time to pull a disappearing act."

"And that's when he changed his name?"

"Correct. He became Stanley Wentworth and headed for Devon. And he'd not been down here long when he met and apparently fell for a café owner's daughter in a little village close to Exeter."

"Celia Richardson?"

"The very one. Although she wasn't Richardson then, of course."

"We know a little about that part of his life then," said Charlie. "But only from Celia's point of view, of course. She never found out why he vanished before their wedding day. There were rumours, of course, but that's it."

"Yes. And, talking to my sources in the West Midlands police force, the rumours are true. His trail had gone completely cold and they might never have found him, except he got in touch with his former mates, with an eye to setting up some of the old tricks down here in the South West. Although the police couldn't find him, the gang members knew roughly where he was. And when the police picked up one of them on suspicion of being involved in the original murder, he turned grass to save his own skin. He tipped off the boys in blue about Stanley's whereabouts. And even with a changed name, it was relatively easy to track down a newcomer in a small community like that."

"And that's when he ran away again?"

"He did. And if he'd just ditched his car and laid low, he'd probably have got away with it."

"His car! I'd forgotten about that. Celia told Annie it was a flashy bright yellow two-seater and his absolute pride and joy."

"Precisely. Stanley headed north, but the police were closing in on him and within a couple of weeks of leaving

Coombesford, they picked him up in Anglesey, attempting to board a ferry to Ireland. Ironically, if he'd headed for London, or Liverpool, any big city really, he'd have been able to stay hidden. But that's the thing about remote areas. Everyone knows your business."

"So, the rumours were true? He went to prison?"

"Yes, he did. Stanley Adams, also known as Stanley Adam Wentworth, served seven years in Winson Green prison for accessory to murder. He got out in 2004, by which time Celia had married Roger Richardson and taken over Cosy Corner from her parents."

"I wonder if he knew that had happened? I wonder if that's why he didn't come back for so many years?"

"Partly, yes, I think it was. According to a mate of a mate who knew him back in those days, he spent a lot of his time in prison talking about Celia and how he was going to go straight when he got out. How he'd head back to Devon and pick up where he left off."

"Goodness knows what he was thinking, then. He obviously didn't know our Celia as well as he thought."

"Precisely. Although, apparently, he returned to Devon as soon as they released him. It was while Celia and Roger were away on holiday, so he didn't see them, but it was clear even to someone with an inflated ego like Stanley's that he'd missed the boat. He headed back to the Midlands and stayed there for the next decade."

"And did he go straight?"

"Not likely. He'd made many contacts while he was in prison. Some of them were very unpleasant characters altogether. He seems to have got involved with several gangs since then; always on the periphery, but with enough contacts and abilities to keep himself popular. He went back to his Mr Fixit role and developed quite a reputation for being able to supply anything people needed–for the right price."

"What went wrong, then?"

"Not sure, really. We're back into the realms of rumour

once more here. I know he kept his nose clean; or should I say, he never got caught. But, in a world where gang rivalry's rife, anyone playing both sides against the middle is bound to come a cropper eventually. And I suspect that's what happened to our Mr Wentworth."

"Do we have any concrete suspects, then? There's an awful lot of supposition in all this, Rohan."

The young Indian nodded and took another sip from his pint.

"I think there are three major groups to think about."

"Okay, talk me through them."

"Right. First, there's a gang based in Handsworth. They're into drugs more than anything else. Anyone who's buying soft or hard drugs in Birmingham or the surrounding region is ultimately getting their gear from those guys. They're in continual battle with a mob from London and another from Swansea. And Stanley helped them get weapons when they needed them. Their second-in-command got shot a couple of months back and the weapon used to kill him was part of a batch Stanley bought off an old army friend of his. The gang claims to have put out a hit on Stanley."

"Okay, that's one group. What's next?"

"Another Birmingham gang, but this time, involved in gambling. They've got the racecourses in England sewn up."

"Shades of *Peaky Blinders*?"

"Exactly. This one's tenuous, but Stanley was married to the daughter of the gang leader. She ran off with someone else a few years back, but it doesn't seem to have worked out. She's no spring chicken, and word on the street has it she was hoping to get back together with our boy. When he disappeared, she appealed to her father, and he put out the word that Stanley was to be found."

"Now that is interesting, Rohan. It would certainly explain Maureen Walsh's arrival in Coombesford. But why kill him?"

"That was my thought, too. Personally, I think that's a

long shot. Unless Stanley didn't fancy returning to wedded bliss and topped himself to get away?"

"But how would he have ended up in the woods in that case?"

"No idea. But I agree it's an unlikely scenario." Rohan paused for breath and took another sip of his drink. "My money's on the Bristol crowd."

"And where do they fit into the picture?"

"That's just it. They don't, at first sight. They hide behind a chain of fine dining establishments, but actually specialise in white-collar crime. Any corruption or embezzlement scam you can mention in the southwest, you can be pretty sure this lot has a hand in it somewhere. And over the past couple of years, they've been expanding northward, trying to increase their influence across the Midlands as well."

"And how would Stanley have been involved with them? What would he be providing for them?"

"Information, rather than hardware, I suspect. He's got– or rather I should say, he had–his finger in so many pies, he knew a bit about everything and everyone. And my contacts suspect he was helping them develop a profitable little blackmail scheme."

"And what went wrong?"

"As far as I can tell, some targets had links to the other two gangs, and things were getting very muddled. Then one of the up-and-coming stars in the Bristol crowd died in a hit-and-run incident. Stanley was one of only three people who knew where the guy was going to be that night. And the other two were family. The finger of suspicion pointed firmly in Stanley's direction. Maybe the family wanted revenge?"

"So all we really know is that for some reason, possibly connected with one of these gangs, Stanley needed to pull another disappearing act?"

"Correct. And that was about the time Simon Mountjoy bought the Village Store. Somehow, they made contact, and

Stanley came back to Coombesford for the third, and as it turns out, the final time."

Rohan swallowed the last of his pint and stood up, pointing to Charlie's half-full glass. "Another one?"

But she looked at her watch and shook her head.

"Sorry, Rohan, but no, I don't have time right now." She stood and gave her old friend a hug. "Look, thanks for all this. It's given me loads to think about. I'll do some digging next time I see the dynamic duo from Exeter nick, see if Harolds knows about all of this. But it certainly looks as though Celia can stop worrying. With all these suspects in the frame, the chances of Roger being involved in Stanley's death are getting slimmer by the minute."

"Ah, yes, Roger." Rohan grinned. "I have a few thoughts about that. I need to check a couple more things, but all I'll say for now is that I doubt Celia has anything to worry about. Not as far as Stanley's murder is concerned, anyway!"

"Sounds intriguing. I look forward to hearing more." Charlie pulled her car keys from her pocket and started walking towards the door. Then she turned back to Rohan. "Are you doing anything tomorrow afternoon?"

"No. Why?"

"Well, we're going up to Fosters Farm to visit Esther Steele. She's worried about her father. Thinks the police might have him in the frame for her mother's killing. We're going to put our heads together to see if we can help her. We might well have something else for you to do."

CHAPTER 27

"So we're looking for information about any strangers in the village? Someone with links to drugs, gambling or white-collar crime." Esther felt her pulse quicken as she looked around the table at her visitors. She'd not felt this sort of excitement for a long time, if ever.

"That's what my investigations suggest, yes," said Rohan. She'd only just met him, but already suspected they were going to be great mates. "Our Mr Stanley Wentworth had a dodgy past and some very unsavoury connections."

"Well, there's one thing about living in a small village. Strangers stand out like a sore thumb. We could ask all the regulars if they've seen anyone they don't recognise hanging around lately." Annie took a sip of tea and bit into a shortbread biscuit. "Yum, these are wonderful, Esther." She swallowed, then went on. "As Charlie said, it looks like Maureen Walsh was telling the truth about why she's come to Coombesford. But I'm still not convinced by the story Daniel Esposito spun us about setting up a fine dining restaurant in the village. Then, of course, there's that young man with the motorbike and those dreadful earrings who's been hanging around for the past couple of weeks." Picking up her biscuit again, she carried on munching, a beatific smile on her face.

"No, I don't buy it." Charlie was shaking her head.

"What don't you buy, Charlie?" asked Esther.

"Well, don't you think it's all a bit too far-fetched? A guy with a criminal record and some very dubious connections hiding away in a little village in Devon. And then getting discovered by one or more of those connections when he appears in a newspaper article. And them coming down here from the Midlands or Bristol to kill him, and drop his body in the woods."

"Hmmm, it does all sound a bit Lee Child, doesn't it?" As an avid reader of thrillers, Esther had every Jack Reacher book on her Kindle and had watched both the films and the TV series as well.

"And it all happens at exactly the same time as another body turns up; a body that's been hidden for more than a quarter of a century." Charlie glanced across at Esther with a look of apology on her face. Esther smiled and waved away her concerns.

"It's okay, Charlie. We have to talk about my mother. That's why you guys are here, after all. But, it's just a coincidence, surely? How could there be any connection between the two murders?"

"I really don't know, Esther. But I always remember what my old group leader used to say back in the day: there's no such thing as a coincidence."

"Of course there is, Charlie," interrupted Annie. "We come across them all the time. You buy a new car, and the very next day, you see someone else with exactly the same model, same colour, everything. Or two people arriving at a party wearing the same dress."

"Those aren't coincidences, Annie. Well, the second one might be, although if they both live in the same area, the chances are they shop in the same stores. And as for the cars, that's called positive reinforcement. Once you've bought a particular item, especially when it's cost the sort of money a new car would, you look for any confirmation that your choice is good. You're looking out for other people who've made the same decision as you. Basic psychology really." Annie looked sceptical, but Charlie carried on speaking. "What we're talking about here is a small village where suddenly, within three days of each other, two bodies turn up, with the only connection between them being they both died under suspicious circumstances. What are the odds of that happening?"

Esther blew out a long, slow breath.

"Well, when you put it like that, I guess you're right."

"I'm sure I'm right. There has to be a connection between the two murders. Someone knew June Steele's body was about to be discovered. And that someone also knew Stanley Wentworth could point the finger at the original murderer. So he had to be silenced." Charlie reached across the table and took Esther's hand. "I'm convinced that in order to solve the latest case, we'll need to solve the earlier one first. If we can find out what happened to your mother all those years ago, it will lead us to Stanley Wentworth's killer as well."

"And the police?"

"The police? Huh. I suspect it's going to take them a lot longer to come to that conclusion. DCI Harolds was in the bar yesterday evening and she told me they were concentrating on Stanley's case. They don't have the resources to deal with two murders at once. And privately, she implied they might never find out what happened to June."

"But that's terrible." Annie was blinking back tears as she turned to her friend. "It must be awful for you and your dad. Fancy thinking all these years she'd deserted you and now finding she was right here in the centre of the village all that time."

"But it's worse than that, guys. I've already had Celia desperate to find proof Roger had nothing to do with Stanley's death. And, Esther, you're worried when the police get around to investigating your mother's murder, they're likely to end up implicating your father." Charlie turned to

Annie and Rohan. "Two of our friends are concerned about people they love being under suspicion."

"We have to help them, Charlie, don't we?"

Charlie nodded slowly.

"Yes, Annie, we do. It's time to get the old team back together." She paused and then grabbed a pad and pencil from the table. "Right, let's write down everything we know about both the victims and their families and friends. And we need to check the exact timings back in 1996. Did Stanley Wentworth leave the village before or after June disappeared?" Esther felt a warm glow of gratitude flow through her as Charlie went on. "I just know if we can find out who killed Esther's mum and why, it'll take us straight to the killer of Stanley Wentworth."

CHAPTER 28

Maureen Walsh closed the door of the bar behind her and slipped across the car park towards the pool of shadow next to the hedge. She held her breath and waited. Her stroll around the village between supper and bedtime had become a nightly habit. And nearly every night, she'd bumped into Amelia Johnson.

The two women hadn't spoken since their first encounter at the viewing point outside Mountjoy Manor. In fact, Amelia barely acknowledged the other woman's presence. But Maureen couldn't shake the feeling she was being followed. And it was time to find out why.

Tonight, however, appeared to be the exception. The door out of The Falls remained resolutely closed and there was no-one on the street either. After about ten minutes, Maureen gave up waiting and leaving the car park, turned right towards the village green.

At the entrance to the church, a powerful wave of floral scents hit her. There was honeysuckle and dog rose growing through the hedgerow enclosing the small graveyard, and the aroma was almost overpowering.

Maureen slipped through the lych-gate, and immediately the rest of the world faded away. She wandered in the gathering gloom, examining the names on the gravestones.

When she came upon a memorial bench near the door to the church, she sat down and lit a cigarette.

At some point soon, she was going to have to make some decisions. She'd come to Devon hoping to reignite her relationship with Stanley Wentworth. But things hadn't worked out as she'd expected. As the man's estranged wife, she'd been told by the police she needed to stay in the village for the moment. And it was certainly a beautiful place. But was it somewhere she wanted to remain long-term?

She was no nearer a decision when she heard a sound that brought chills to her, and she shivered. There were soft footsteps on the gravel around the side of the church. She wasn't alone. But from the sound of it, whoever was there didn't want to be seen.

"Hello. Is anyone there?" she called. The sounds stopped and total silence enveloped her. She stood and started walking towards the gate. The footsteps began once again. She stopped. They stopped. She began again, they began again.

Maureen lost it. She dashed for the gate, wrenched it open, and shot out onto the village green. There was no-one around. The village looked deserted. Completely spooked by now, she started running again and headed for The Falls. She was very grateful she'd worn trainers tonight, rather than her more normal high heels.

She saw no-one in the time it took her to reach the car park and finally she felt safe enough to stop running and catch her breath. As her heart gradually slowed down, she scolded herself. It wasn't normal for her to take fright like that. And looking back up the lane, there was no-one in sight. She must have imagined it. How could she, a tough cookie, who'd spent many a night in the old graveyard with her friends back in Ireland, and frequently walked the streets of London or Birmingham on her own, take fright in a little churchyard in Devon? Devon, of all places! It was hardly a hotbed of crime. She sat on the little bench on the edge of the car park and smoked another cigarette. She didn't think she'd tell Charlie or Annie about what had happened on her walk. They'd think she was daft.

Finishing her cigarette, she rose and started walking across the car park towards the bar. Lights were spilling from the windows, and she could see the place had got much busier since she'd gone out for her walk. The car park seemed to be full. In the three spaces against the fence, she noticed a large silver 4x4 parked side by side with a muddy old Defender Land Rover. To one side, she spotted a flashy-looking motor cycle, black with gold and red flames licking the petrol tanks.

The pub was a converted Devon long house with a thatched roof. The walls were brilliant white and the spotlights in the car park played on the paintwork. She watched, fascinated, as her shadow gradually grew as she approached the building. Then her blood froze as a second shadow joined hers. Someone was walking across the car park behind her. At that moment, the shadow raised an arm, an arm holding a stick or club angled above its head. As the arm descended, Maureen Walsh screamed.

CHAPTER 29

Despite the noise in the bar, everyone heard the screaming from the car park. There was an instant of paralysed silence. Then Charlie, who was collecting empties, dropped her tray on the nearest table and sprinted for the door, closely followed by several of the regulars.

The screaming had stopped and at first, the car park appeared to be empty. Then someone pointed towards a pool of shadow by the hedge.

"Over there."

Charlie hurried over. It was a woman, lying at a strange angle, with her arms flung above her head as though trying to stop her fall. Or protect herself, maybe. A woman that Charlie knew very well indeed.

Annie was standing at the door of the pub. Charlie looked back at her and shook her head.

"You'll need to call the police, Annie. It's Amelia Johnson. I'm afraid she's dead. It looks like someone attacked her."

At that moment, there was a groan from behind one of the nearby cars. Everyone looked up as Maureen Walsh stumbled to her feet. There was a gash down the side of her head and a graze on her knee.

Someone helped her to stand and held on to her.

"What happened, Maureen?" asked Charlie. "Were you attacked as well?"

Maureen shook her head, then grimaced and put her hands to her temples.

"Ouch. No, I fell and must have hit my head on the corner of the car. I was running away. He was just a shadow, and I thought he was right behind me. I screamed, ran, slipped, and that's all I can remember." At that moment, she caught sight of Amelia's body. Her hands flew to her mouth. "My God. Is that Amelia? How terrible."

"Did you see who it was?" asked Charlie. Maureen pursed her lips and shook her head slowly.

"No. I saw a shadow on the wall, raising a club or something. I thought he was after me and I just ran. After I fell, I heard a thud and a crash. I guess that must have been when he hit her."

"Well, let's get you inside," said Annie, taking Maureen by the arm. "The police will want to talk to you, but you can come and sit in the bar until they arrive."

Maureen looked back across the car park to where Amelia's body lay.

"It doesn't seem right to just leave her lying there…"

"We won't do that," said Charlie. "I'll stay and watch over her until they arrive. You go inside with Annie." She raised her voice. "Back inside, everyone, please. This is a crime scene. The police won't want you all trampling over it."

As the two women walked back into the pub, the rest of the crowd tagged along behind them, leaving Charlie on her own, leaning against the porch. She stared across the car park. Opposite her she could see a large silver 4x4. So Daniel Esposito was still here somewhere. Although she didn't remember seeing him in the crowd that came outside after Maureen screamed. Next to his vehicle was a muddy old Land Rover. And next to that was the only space in the place. She just hoped when the police arrived, they'd be able to squeeze their squad car in there. But she guessed if they couldn't, they'd just park in the middle of the car park, blocking people in and announcing there was trouble at The Falls. Not that it mattered. There were enough people around who'd seen what happened. The news would've travelled across the whole of the village – if not to Plymouth and Exeter – by now.

CHAPTER 30

The crime scene investigator had told DCI Harolds that by the time the police had secured the scene, taken preliminary details and removed the body, it was nearly dawn. They'd spoken to all the people who'd been in the bar at the time of the incident, and taken their names, where they'd been when they heard the scream, and who they'd been talking to. Then they'd sent them home, with a warning to come back the next morning for formal interviews. A few grumbled because it meant they'd be late for work, but most seemed willing, if not eager, to take part in a murder investigation.

"Getting to be a bit of a habit, isn't it, Charlie?" the DCI said as she settled herself on a stool at the bar. Charlie opened her mouth and looked as though she was about to object, but the detective flapped her hands at her and smiled her steely smile, which people had told her never quite reached her eyes. "It's alright. There're dozens of witnesses who swear you were in the bar collecting glasses when they heard the scream." She sighed. "I only wish their recollection of all the other people was as definite. Everyone remembers someone they were talking to. But everyone's memories seem to differ."

"We understand Ms Walsh is staying here, Charlie, is that

right?" said DS Smith. It was a rhetorical question, as their briefing had included the fact that Maureen had finally gone to bed around 4am. Plus, they'd already spoken to her in relation to her husband's murder.

"Maureen? Yes, that's right. But she's not up yet. She was so upset by what happened that we thought we'd let her sleep on. She missed breakfast; Annie's just about to take a tray up to her."

"Perhaps she could ask her to get dressed and come down as soon as she's eaten, please? She appears to be the nearest thing we have to a witness to the death. And if you'd be so good as to show us to our room, we'll get set up."

Charlie led the two detectives upstairs to an empty room—the same one they'd occupied three years before when investigating Simon Mountjoy's murder.

"It won't take long to settle ourselves in," said DCI Harolds, "so you can send Ms Walsh in as soon as she's up and about."

Andrea Harolds propped her elbows on the table and steepled her index fingers in front of her pursed lips as she stared silently at the woman in front of her.

Maureen Walsh was pale, and the remains of yesterday's mascara lay in smudges around her eyes. Her crumpled blouse didn't match the slacks she was wearing over bare feet and thin rubber thong sandals. She looked as though she needed a decent night's sleep, a good wash, and a fresh outfit. Which was hardly surprising for a woman who'd witnessed a murder in the car park, had spent half the night sitting up waiting for the police to talk to her, and had barely had six hours sleep. So, yes, her appearance was perfectly understandable, thought the DCI. But was there something else going on here, something the woman in front of her desperately wanted to hide?

"How are you feeling this morning, Ms Walsh?" Harolds asked, putting on what she knew her colleagues called her 'pretend I care' face. The woman opposite her smiled wanly, although her eyes filled with unshed tears.

"I'm doing okay, thank you, Detective Chief Inspector," was the whispered response.

"Ms Walsh, I know you told the uniformed officers this last night, but do you think you could bear to go through what happened, just one more time? It will really help with our investigations."

Maureen pulled a tissue from out of her cleavage and mopped at her eyes. Then she nodded her head and began speaking in a tiny voice.

"I was walking across the car park. I was watching my shadow grow on the wall in front of me. The spotlights, you know?" Harolds nodded. She'd been told all about the lighting in the car park, how some places, including the white walls of the pub, were brilliantly lit up and how other parts were pools of darkness. "Then suddenly, there was a second shadow right behind me—or at least, that's what it looked like. And he was raising his arm with something in it. It looked like a club, like a rounders' bat, or something of that sort. I thought he was attacking me, so I just screamed and ran. But I caught my foot on something and fell against a car. It winded me, but I crawled around the side of the car, where it was darker, and hid. And that's when I heard it."

"Heard what, Ms Walsh?" prompted DS Smith. The woman was obviously trying to contain her tears once more.

"I heard a thud and a crash. Like someone being hit and falling."

"And after that?"

"Then it all went quiet. I thought he was coming to look for me. I just curled up and held my breath. Then everyone piled out of the pub and I knew I was safe."

DCI Harolds regarded the woman steadily before asking her next question.

"Did you see anyone in the car park when you first arrived? Did you see Amelia Johnson, for example?"

"No, no-one." She paused. "I'd been running and sat down on the bench by the road to get my breath back and have a cigarette." She pulled a face. "Yes, I know it's a filthy habit and I'm trying to give up…" Harolds waved a hand to show this was of no interest to her and she wasn't about to judge. If Maureen Walsh knew her better, she'd be aware the DCI was partial to the odd cigarillo after dinner, anyway. But this wasn't a piece of information she was going to share. Especially when her oh-so-judgmental sergeant was in the room. She gestured for the woman to continue. "It was completely silent. I heard no-one and saw no-one. And I was on the lookout, so would have seen anyone if they'd been around."

"Why was that, Ms Walsh?" DS Smith asked. "Why were you making a point of looking around?"

The woman gave a nervous laugh.

"You're going to think me silly," she said. "But I'd been walking around the churchyard, and I heard footsteps. They seemed to follow me. Every time I moved, they moved. But every time I stopped, they stopped."

"What did you do?"

"Well, I called out to see if anyone was there, but there was no answer. And then I got spooked, I don't mind telling you. I took off fast and ran all the way from the churchyard to the car park." She paused and smiled at them. "It might not look like it now, Detectives, but I used to be a great little runner when I was a teenager. Ran for the county, I did. But that's all a long time ago. I've not run for more than a bus in thirty years or more!"

"But you don't know who was in the churchyard with you?"

"Absolutely not. I saw no-one. And when I got to the car park, I looked back and the lane and the green were both completely empty. And so was the car park. At least, that's what I thought. Although I was wrong, wasn't I?" Her lip trembled, and a tear spilled from her eye and ran down her cheek.

DCI Harolds made a final note on her pad and then clicked the top of her pen.

"All right, Ms Walsh. We'll leave it there for now. But we may need to talk to you again. Have you decided how long you're planning on staying in Coombesford?"

"To be honest, DCI Harolds, I'm not sure what I'm planning to do. As you know, I came to see Stanley Wentworth, my husband. And I'd not made plans past that point. Now he's dead. I don't know what to do next. I can't go back to…" She shook her head and took a deep breath. "Let's just say I'm considering my options."

"Well, do us a favour, Ms Walsh, will you? Book yourself in here for a few more days. Just until we get a clearer view of things."

"Yes. Yes, of course, if you think it'll help the investigation."

Maureen smiled, shook hands with each of the detectives and left the room, with slightly more of a spring in her step than when she'd arrived thirty minutes earlier.

"What are you thinking, boss?" asked DS Smith.

"Not sure, Derek. Not sure at all. By her own admission, there was no-one else in the car park apart from her and Amelia Johnson. She could have done the deed and then screamed and thrown herself into that dark corner to put us off the scent."

"But this was a vicious attack. Surely it had to be a man who did it?"

"Not necessarily. Anyone swinging a club at the right angle can get a pretty solid blow in. And Maureen Walsh is a heftily built woman. I reckon she could pack quite a punch if she put her mind to it."

"But why? What's the connection between the two women?" Smith paused and then clicked his fingers. "Of course. Stanley Wentworth. The Village Store. Amelia Johnson worked for him."

"And if the former Mrs Wentworth was hoping for another shot at their marriage, then having an attractive woman like Amelia Johnson around might be very inconvenient."

"Yet Wentworth is dead as well."

"Maybe Walsh suspected Johnson was involved in his death?"

"Or Walsh killed Wentworth because he wouldn't leave Johnson for her–and then went back for Johnson in revenge."

The two detectives looked at each other in silence for a few minutes. Then Andrea Harolds shook her head and smiled. "It's a nice theory, Derek, but that's all it is for now; a theory. We need some evidence." She picked up her notepad and stuffed it in her bag. "Time to do some more digging into all their pasts, I think. I reckon that's where we'll find the answers to all this. Plus, we still need to interview Mr Daniel Esposito. Find out his connection to Wentworth and the Village Store."

"And Maureen Walsh?"

"Oh, we need to make sure we monitor her for the moment. Have a word with Charlie and Annie, would you? Ask them to let us know the minute Ms Walsh makes any moves towards leaving Coombesford. I think we'll need to be talking to her again before this is all over."

CHAPTER 31

DS Derek Smith yawned hugely and groaned. He'd been going over these witness statements for hours, reading, re-reading. And he'd come up with nothing so far. Yet his boss said she knew there was something in there. Something they'd missed. And over the past four years he'd been working for DCI Andrea Harolds, he'd learned to trust her instincts. He glanced at the clock. Twenty past six. He'd promised his wife he'd be home in time to read the kids a bedtime story tonight. But maybe if he just went through the reports one more time…

And fifty-five minutes later, it hit him. The thing that had been rankling with him all day. The last piece in the jigsaw. He picked up the phone.

"Boss, I think I've found our missing link…"

"Ms Walsh, can you just run through what you saw in the car park one more time? What did you notice about the vehicles when you walked through? Before you saw the shadow and started running?"

"Well, let me see. The car park was full. There were no empty spaces at all. A mixture of cars, most of which I didn't take any notice of."

"In your original statement, you described three vehicles

in particular?"

"Oh, yes, I noticed them especially, they were such a contrast. In those three spaces to the side there. A large silver 4x4; a Land Rover Discovery, I believe. And next to it, a dirty old Defender. It amused me the two had the same maker's badge but were so very different."

DS Smith held his breath.

"And next to them, a black motorbike with orange and red flames painted on it."

"I'd like you to think back, Charlie, to what you saw while you were waiting for the police and the ambulance to arrive that night. I want to check something in your statement."

"Sure thing, DS Smith. I didn't want to stand too close to the body. It's not the sort of sight you want to spend too much time with, is it? But I needed to be where I could see her. To make sure no-one disturbed her, you understand. So I strolled across to the row of spaces on the side there. I leaned up against the Land Rover."

"Which one?"

"Oh, the old muddy one, of course. I knew the owner of that wouldn't have bothered to put the alarm on. He never worries about anyone stealing his vehicle. I reckon he'd be glad if they did. It would save him from giving it its quarterly wash! And I didn't want to lean against the big silver one. I had a suspicion Mr Esposito would have set his alarm, and I thought we could do without more drama for one night."

"And what about the third space in the row?"

"The one closest to the road? Oh, that one was empty."

"You're sure about that?"

"Absolutely positive. I remember thinking it was a good job it was clear otherwise there'd be nowhere for the police car to park."

Andrea Harolds and Derek Smith put down the lists they had been going through and grinned at each other.

"Charlie has him on her list of drinkers from earlier in the evening," said the DCI.

"But he's not in the crowd the plods rounded up afterwards."

"We assumed he'd left before this all kicked off…"

"But Maureen Walsh's statement puts him, or at least his motorbike, still here just before the attack. But how did he get away with no-one hearing him?"

"I imagine he just pushed the bike up the drive while everyone was concentrating on Amelia, then started it up when he was clear of here."

"Hang on a minute." The DS picked up the pile of statements and riffled through them. "I thought so. One person reported hearing a car backfiring in the distance while they were helping Ms Walsh into the pub. What if that wasn't a car backfiring at all? What if it was a motorbike being fired up and ridden away?"

"Do we know where Rory Black's staying?"

"Charlie said he's staying in Teignmouth, boss. At Mrs Winterbotham's B&B just off the seafront."

"Well, what are we waiting for? Time to go to the seaside, sergeant."

CHAPTER 32

But when the police arrived at the B&B, they found Rory Black's room deserted. The landlady told them her young lodger had disappeared on his bike two days ago and she hadn't seen him since. She thought she'd heard him coming in late that same night, but when she'd knocked on his door the next morning, there was no sign of him. She wasn't a happy bunny. He'd left the room in quite a state, with torn papers all over the place, empty fish and chip boxes and a half-eaten pizza on the table, together with empty beer cans. And mixed with the odour of stale beer and greasy food was another smell with which the detectives were very familiar. Black had been smoking in his room; despite the huge No Smoking notice on the back of the door. And it didn't smell like tobacco he'd been using.

"I keep a nice clean establishment here," the old woman complained. "This room stinks. I'll have to leave it for a couple of days before I can let it again."

DCI Harolds looked around at the faded curtains and bedclothes, the mismatched furniture and worn carpet, and raised an eyebrow at DS Smith. It would take more than a couple of days of airing to make this room habitable in her eyes.

"Okay, Mrs Winterbotham. Why don't you leave us to

it? I'm sure you've got other things to be doing. We'll give you a shout when we're leaving." She gently eased the woman across the room, pushed her back onto the landing, and closed the door in her face. "Right, DS Smith, let's see what Mr Black's room can tell us, shall we?"

Their search revealed an envelope with scrawled directions from Teignmouth to Coombesford, a book of matches from a nightclub in Coventry, and very little else. Smith found a plastic bag in the bottom of the wardrobe and, splitting it open, spread it across the table, pushing the empty boxes and beer cans into the sink, out of the way. Then, with a grimace of disgust, he upended the plastic swing top bin onto the table and began sorting through the detritus, wearing a pair of rubber gloves. There were more beer cans; more fish and chip boxes, an empty hair gel container, and just before he was about to give up, a scrap of torn up paper.

"Looks like an envelope," he said, holding it up. The DCI pulled on her own pair of gloves and the two began a fingertip search of the pile of rubbish. And in the end, their diligence brought its reward.

"27 Hill View, Coombesford, TQ13 0ZZ."

"That sounds familiar," said Smith.

"It should do. It's the address of the Village Store. The one where both Stanley Wentworth and Amelia Johnson worked. I think we've got him, DS Smith. All we have to do now is find him."

It took another three days in the end to catch up with Rory Black. They found his motorbike abandoned in the car park of Exeter St David's Station, covered in parking tickets. CCTV footage showed him buying a train ticket first thing on the morning after the murder and boarding a train for the Midlands. And at Birmingham New Street, they spotted him transferring to a train for Coventry. It seemed like Rory Black had gone home. And the local police in Coventry traced him pretty quickly to one of his old haunts, a snooker hall in the shady end of the city. DCI Andrea Harolds and DS Derek Smith drove up early the next morning to interview him.

CHAPTER 33

"Come on, Mr Black," said Harolds, letting a note of exasperation creep into her voice, much as she tried to hide it, "we know you've been staying in Teignmouth for the past couple of weeks. We know you were in Coombesford. We've got CCTV footage of you hanging around the Village Store almost daily. Witnesses can place you in The Falls on the evening of the murder. But by the time the police arrived to interview everyone, you'd left. Why was that?"

Black's skin was pale and blotchy. He'd chewed his filthy fingernails to the quick. And he smelt like he hadn't had a shower for days. He shook his head.

"I don't know nothing about no murder! Okay, so I stopped in for a drink, but I left quite early. I was coming back home the next day. I needed to get back to the B&B to pack."

"But we have a credible witness who saw your bike in the car park immediately after the murder took place. You couldn't have left earlier, unless you walked back to Teignmouth, that is. Yet, a few minutes later, it was gone. And more than one person heard you ride away when they were all in the car park looking after Maureen Walsh. How can you explain that?"

"And you didn't tell your landlady you were leaving

Teignmouth, did you, Rory? Then you ditched your bike in Exeter and got on a train. Now why did you leave such a valuable bike behind? Why not ride it back to the Midlands?"

"Could it be because the bike didn't belong to Mr Black, do you think, boss?" asked DS Smith with a sly grin. Black looked up in surprise. "Yes, we looked into that motor bike of yours. Couldn't understand why anyone would dump such a beautiful machine. Turns out the owner reported it stolen from a service station on the M5 at the end of August."

"Just over two weeks ago, Rory. Right before you arrived in Devon, and started hanging around Coombesford. So why don't you do us all a favour and tell us what happened?"

The young man stared at them defiantly for a while, then just as though someone had pricked him with a pin, he seemed to collapse in on himself.

"She was my mother," he whispered. "She was my mother, but she didn't want to know me." And he burst into tears.

DCI Harolds looked at her sergeant with a mixture of surprise and triumph in her look. Then she turned to the young man and patted him on the arm.

"Why don't you start at the beginning," she said.

"I've always known my parents adopted me as a baby," he said, "and that I wasn't really welcome in their home."

"So why…?" began DS Smith, but Harolds held up a finger to stop him from interrupting. She had a feeling if they just kept quiet, they were going to get the complete story.

"Amelia Johnson was my birth mother. She gave me up for adoption when I was just a few days old. My adoptive parents were Susan and Michael Black, a couple who had no kids. He was okay most of the time. Although he was totally under Susan's thumb. She was a real bitch. Believed in the old saying 'spare the rod, spoil the child' and certainly applied that saying—to me, at least.

"They'd been married for over ten years when I was born. They'd been unable to have any children, and time was running out for Susan. So they adopted me. And I think they were okay for the first couple of years. Then, when I was two, Susan finally got pregnant. And everything changed. In fact, one of my earliest memories was being shut out on the landing when Michael saw his wife and met their son for the first time. Michael Junior they called him, or Mickey for short."

"And what happened after that?"

"Well, let's just say they made it quite clear I was very much the second-class citizen in that family. They excluded me from treats and left me to my own devices much of the time. In fact, I think if they could've sent me back, they would've done. Susan once told me she wished I'd been a foster child, rather than adopted, because then they could've put me in a children's home!"

Andrea Harolds felt her heart squeeze. She knew the young man in front of her was certainly a criminal–they'd had a long talk with the local police when they arrived at the station–and it was looking like he was a killer as well. But, for a moment, all she could think about was a small boy, through no fault of his own, an unwanted outsider right from when he was a toddler. She pushed that thought away as Black carried on talking.

"I learned pretty young to look after myself. And I got by, making myself as invisible as possible. I'd do my chores, ask for nothing from them–and receive it most of the time. As soon as I could, when I was seventeen, I left school and home at the same time.

"All the time I was growing up, I gave very little thought to my birth mother. Then last year, I saw this programme on the box, about finding long-lost relatives, and I got to thinking: who was she and why had she given me up?"

"You researched her?"

"That's right. I went back to the neighbourhood where I grew up. I knew Michael Black drank occasionally in The

Red Lion. I hung around for a few days and, sure enough, he turned up. He could remember my birth mother's name and told me she was a single mum, recently divorced."

"And how did you find her?"

The young man looked shifty at that.

"Let's just say I've got some mates... I got her name and found out she was living in Devon. So I went down to meet her."

"And was she pleased to see you?"

"Not at all. She was horrified. I went to see her earlier that day at her place. I'd assumed she gave me up because she had no money and couldn't cope. But she soon put me straight on that. Turns out she'd got plenty of money from her divorce settlement. No, she gave me up because she didn't want to be saddled with a child. Those were her exact words. 'I had no wish to be saddled with a child then,' she said, 'and I don't feel any different now. So I suggest you turn around and go back to the big city where you came from.' Then she threw me out."

"Not a nice thing to hear."

"Not at all. That night in the pub, I sat and watched her laughing and drinking with friends. Then when that other woman went out for a walk, she followed her."

"Maureen Walsh?"

"Yeah, that's right, the loud Irish one. I went after them. Watched my mother stalking Maureen Walsh, hiding from her and trying to spook her in the churchyard and then creeping back to the car park and lying in wait for her. And she seemed so awful. I couldn't believe this was the woman I'd spent so long looking for. And she didn't want to know me."

"And that's why you attacked her?"

Black nodded.

"For the tape, Mr Black?"

"Yes." His voice came out as a broken whisper and he cleared his throat and tried again. "Yes, I stumbled over a piece of fence post lying on the ground. And I just grabbed it and swung it at her. Didn't know I'd killed her. I just felt so betrayed. I thought I'd disappear and no-one would know who'd done it. But that Maureen Walsh screamed, and everything went crazy. I hid in the shadows until everyone was busy looking after the two women, then I just pushed my bike up onto the road, started the engine and left."

"Okay, Mr Black. Now tell us about Stanley Wentworth. What did he do that made you want to kill him?"

The young man's head shot up, and he looked at the two detectives in alarm.

"Stanley who?"

"Stanley Wentworth. Amelia's boss at the Village Store. The man you killed and left in Stover Country Park."

Rory Black jumped up from the table and backed away from them, shaking his head.

"No. No. I didn't mean to kill my mother, and I certainly didn't kill anyone else. I've never heard of Stanley Wentworth. You can't pin that on me."

CHAPTER 34

DS Smith took an instant dislike to Daniel Esposito. It wasn't just his physique: broad shoulders and a narrow waist that made him look imposing, even though he was well below average height. Nor that his clothes probably cost at least a couple of months' salary for a detective sergeant. Or that the car he jumped out of was way above the standard the DS could ever hope to afford. Well, it was all of these things, if he was honest. But mostly it was the air of entitlement, the smug smile and the appearance of doing them a favour by coming in to be interviewed at all.

DS Smith hoped fervently they would find something to charge this horrible little man with.

"Mr Esposito," began DCI Harolds, "have you ever visited the Village Store here in Coombesford?"

"You obviously know I have," was the lazy reply. Esposito was leaning back in his chair with one elegantly clad leg hooked over the other. "Otherwise, why am I here?"

"Could you answer the question, please, sir?" snapped Smith. Esposito smirked at him and shrugged.

"Yes, I visited the Village Store about two weeks ago."

"To see Mr Stanley Wentworth?"

"Correct."

"And why was that?"

"We're old friends. I'm working in the area. I thought I'd drop in and say hello."

"And was he pleased to see you?"

"Why wouldn't he be?"

"Isn't it true to say that he was most unhappy to see you and that you argued in the shop?"

Esposito shrugged.

"You obviously had the chance to talk to the attractive redhead before she got herself killed too. So, yes, we argued. He owed me money, quite a lot of money, from a long time ago. I wanted it back. He was trying to change my mind."

"When you say a lot of money, Mr Esposito, how much are we talking about?"

"Fifty thousand, give or take."

DS Smith let out a whistle.

"That's a sum worth killing for, wouldn't you say, boss?" But before the DCI could respond, Esposito planted both feet firmly on the floor, sat up straight, and banged both hands on the table that separated him from the two detectives.

"This is ridiculous. He owed me money. He was going to pay me back. Now he can't, because he's dead. Why on earth would I kill him?"

"But we only have your word for it he was going to pay you back," said Harolds. "Do you have any proof?"

"Actually, I do." Esposito reached down to the snakeskin briefcase at his feet and, snapping it open, pulled out a sheaf of papers. "Here, here's the agreement he signed. Five thousand a month for the next ten months, plus an extra payment as a penalty for defaulting on the original loan. Signed by Stanley Wentworth." He flipped through the papers and pulled out a printout. "And here's a copy of my bank statement." He pointed to an entry from the end of the previous week. "See, he deposited the first instalment the day of our meeting." He threw the papers down on the table and sat back in his chair once again. "I can assure you detectives, whoever killed Stanley Wentworth, it wasn't me!"

CHAPTER 35

It was half past five. People were drifting into The Falls for a quick pint on the way home – or the start of a long evening's drinking in some cases. DCI Harolds and DS Smith walked in to the bar.

"Can we have a quick word, Charlie?" said the DCI. "We'll not keep you long."

Charlie raised her eyes at Rohan, who was sitting on the customer side of the bar for a change. He grinned and slid off his stool.

"I've got this, mate. You go chat with the nice police officers. Just remember, you owe me."

Charlie led the two detectives into the restaurant section, which was still completely empty. Catching sight of Annie in the corridor from the kitchen, she beckoned for her to join them.

As soon as the four of them had sat down, DCI Harolds began.

"I wanted to let you know we've arrested Rory Black for the killing of Amelia Johnson. Your information was very helpful, Charlie. Mind you, it took a while. We tracked him back to his B&B in Teignmouth. He'd gone back there to pick up his stuff, then hightailed it back to the Midlands. If you'd not been able to describe the bike in such great detail, we'd probably have lost him."

"Although he wouldn't have got very far too quickly," said Charlie with a grin. "That's a bike that looks tough, but it's a big softie underneath."

"Which could be why he dumped it in Exeter and took the train home."

"Still, it's good you made an arrest so quickly," said Annie. "Is it going to be difficult to make a case against him?"

"Not difficult at all. Easy, in fact." DS Smith gave a snort of laughter. "He confessed. Tried to bluff his way out of it initially, and to be fair, a lot of what we had was circumstantial. But he didn't seem to realise that. In the end, he just folded. Seemed relieved to get it off his chest, to be honest."

"But why? Why would he come all this way to kill a stranger like that?"

"She wasn't a stranger to him. Not really, although he'd not seen her since he was a baby. Turns out she was his mother!"

"What? Amelia? But she never mentioned she had any kids. She told us her marriage was very short-lived and implied she'd stayed footloose and fancy free ever since."

"Well, that's probably true. Apparently, she didn't find out she was pregnant until after she'd deserted her husband. And she didn't want to go back to him just for the sake of the child. After he was born, she had him adopted. And then she wrote him out of her history. She appears to have forgotten all about him."

"But that's terrible. How could any mother do that?" Annie's eyes filled with tears, and Charlie flashed her a sympathetic smile..

"I'm sorry to say it happens far too often," continued DCI Harolds. "Usually, the young mother realises she can't look after her child. She reckons if she gives him or her away as a baby, there's more chance of adoption and a stable upbringing. If she tries to bring them up herself and fails, social services will get involved. That way, the child is more likely to end up in a variety of foster homes or a children's home."

"And that's why Amelia did it?"

"Well, so Rory thought, anyway. He tracked down his birth mother a while back and came down here to get to know her. Apparently, his adoptive parents were not as nice to him as they might have been, and he ran away as soon as he could.

"He spent time watching Ms Johnson, checking out her routine. He concluded she was a lot better off than the impoverished young divorcee who'd given him up at birth. So he introduced himself to her."

"What went wrong, then?"

"She laughed in his face. Told him to sling his hook! It would appear Ms Amelia Johnson had plenty of money when she got divorced. She'd sewn up her husband in a sweet prenup deal that meant she got pretty much everything. No, she put the baby up for adoption because she wasn't interested in being a parent, full stop. She'd never wanted kids—and that hadn't changed over the years."

"So seeing a young man on her doorstep would be quite jarring?" asked Charlie. "Especially if he thought they could make a go of it as mother and son."

"Precisely. He turned up with flowers and a big smile. And she properly burst his bubble."

"Well, that's not a nice thing for Amelia to do. But she didn't deserve to die because of that, did she?"

"No, she didn't, Annie. She certainly didn't. Black says he drove around for hours after she gave him the brush-off, then finally came back to the village hoping to make her change her mind. He'd parked in the car park here and come in for some Dutch courage. Amelia was in the bar, too, but she just blanked him. When she left, he followed her and watched her play some pretty mean tricks on Maureen Walsh. Black says in the end, he just lost it."

Charlie tapped the table with her fingernail.

"So he didn't plan that murder. But what about Stanley Wentworth? Where does he come into the picture? Two killings within a few days of each other. There must be a link. There can't be two different murderers here, can there?"

The DCI nodded.

"That's our thinking, too. Young Black had been around the village nearly a week by the time Stanley died. We think maybe Black approached him as Amelia's boss. Asked him to intercede for him."

"Or maybe he was jealous of Stanley. He got to spend far more time with Rory's mother than Rory ever did. Jealousy can do strange things to a person."

"Yes, it can, you're right, Charlie. Plus, there's the fact that Stanley Wentworth is also from Coventry, so they may well have known each other in a previous life." The DCI blew out her bottom lip and shrugged. "But young Black is absolutely adamant he had nothing to do with Stanley Wentworth's death. He swears he only heard about it when he saw us picking up Amelia that day to identify the body."

"And do you believe him?" asked Charlie.

"No, of course we don't," scoffed DS Smith. "If he's guilty of one, he has to be guilty of both. As you say, Charlie, this place is too small to harbour two killers at the same time." He licked his lips and looked longingly at the bar. "You mark my words, ladies. Young Rory Black is guilty. And we're going to prove it. Someone will know something and we'll find it. It's only a matter of time."

CHAPTER 36

Rohan Banerjee was delighted to see Charlie leaning against the railing overlooking the beach next to Teignmouth pier when he arrived at the promenade for his daily run. Business wasn't wonderful at the moment, and Rohan was getting worried. He knew he could rely on his friends in Coombesford to keep him busy, but much as he enjoyed serving behind the counter at Cosy Corner on Celia's busy days, or pulling pints at The Falls, that wasn't what he'd come down to the southwest for. He didn't want to have to give up the private investigative work, but searching for the odd missing dog or errant husband wouldn't pay his rent for him.

"Hi, Charlie, come to join me for a run, have you? Going to work off some of that spare tyre?" He ducked away from his friend as she pretended to take a swing at him. Charlie wasn't as trim as she'd been when he first met her, but that was twenty-odd years ago. And she was living a quieter life now than before. Plus, there was Annie's cooking to consider. Rohan always enjoyed being invited to eat at The Falls when Annie McLeod was on kitchen duty.

"Not today, Rohan. I will start running with you again, I promise, as soon as the season quietens down."

"Yeah, yeah. I believe you." He did a couple of stretches

and ran on the spot to warm himself up. "So what brings you down here, then?"

"I've got another job for you. You may need to pull in a few favours, though."

"Sounds intriguing. What do you need?"

Charlie handed him a photograph of Amelia Johnson.

"That's the woman who was killed last week in your car park, isn't it? I've seen her in the bar once or twice. Bit of a stunner, with that red hair."

"That's the one."

"But I thought the police had already caught her killer?"

"Well, yes, they have. They've got a confession, too. That young guy with the motorbike, Rory Black. Says she was his birth mother. But he's denying any knowledge of Stanley Wentworth or who killed him."

"Tell me; why do you want to look into Amelia Johnson's background?"

"Because I think we're missing something, Rohan. It can't be a coincidence that Amelia and Stanley died within days of each other. She'd only been working for him for four years, and before the shop opened, he hadn't been in the village, or anywhere near here for years. The police are looking into his background. But I think we need to know more about her."

"Anything in particular?"

"Well, according to DCI Harolds, Black knows nothing about his father and hasn't bothered to track him down. I'd like you to see if you could do that. Maybe he'll be able to shed some light on this whole matter."

"Okay, Charlie, I'll see what I can do." Rohan finished stretching and reached out his hand to bump fists. "Right, if you're sure you won't join me, I'm going to get moving. I'll start on this later this morning and let you know when I've something to report."

CHAPTER 37

"This must have been a wonderful place to grow up in," said Annie, putting her mug back on the table and gesturing out of the window.

Esther nodded her head and smiled.

"Oh, it was, Annie; it certainly was. Things were so different when Mum was around. That was before she got ill. And before my accident too, of course."

The two women were sitting in Esther's studio, a large, sunny space occupying the front of the building to the left of the main entrance door. It was mid-morning when Annie had arrived to collect Suzy's birthday present. It hadn't been difficult for Esther to persuade her to agree to stop for a quick drink and a chat, although she said she needed to be back at The Falls within the hour to get ready for the lunchtime trade.

Esther had displayed the picture on her easel, turned so the sun shining through the brightly polished windows lit it beautifully. It showed her interpretation of the party celebrating the adventurers' return to Hobbiton after the destruction of the One Ring. Sam Gamgee was dancing with Rosie, the young hobbit that was to become his wife, surrounded by crowds of laughing friends and neighbours. In the sky above them, one of Gandalf's magic fireworks had just burst into life. But Rosie's face was Suzy's. It was a delightful composition, and Esther felt a warm glow of satisfaction when Annie said her daughter would love it.

"Tell me a bit about your life back then," Annie said.

"Well, during the summer months, I lived outside–we all did, really. Mum and Dad were always laughing and joking. They were such fun to be with." She smiled at the sceptical look on Annie's face and nodded vigorously. "Yes, really. Dad wasn't always the grumpy person people think he is– and in fact, he's rarely grumpy with me, even now. But things changed when Mum started getting ill…" She paused, then gave herself a mental shake and carried on. "There were lots of people working on the farm, of course, but at busy times, especially around harvest, everyone had to pitch in. Mum would pack us some sandwiches for lunch and we'd head down to the fields mid-morning and not come home until dusk. I had so much fun!"

"Sounds like it. I grew up on Skye, but in a fishing village rather than a farming community. We were also outside all day. Summers seemed to go on forever when we were children, didn't they?"

"Indeed. But, to be honest, I think it was the winters I loved even more. Once the harvest was in, and the ploughing done, ready for the next year's crop, there wasn't much to do until lambing started. Dad would do the milking morning and evening; and my job was to collect the eggs every day, but for the rest of the time, we all huddled up in here out of the cold. Mum did loads of cooking: Christmas puddings, mincemeat, fruit cakes flavoured with spiced rum. And preserving, of course. She used to make pickles and chutneys with all the leftover vegetables. We had home-grown produce all year around."

"Pickled onions!" said Annie. "My gran used to make them each autumn, and we only opened the jar on Christmas night to eat them with the cold turkey sandwiches." She pulled a face. "I couldn't stand the taste of them at any other time of the year, but somehow they tasted wonderful on that one special night."

"I used to love everything about Christmas," said Esther. "Still do, in fact, although we're not so sociable these days as we used to be. Dad would bring up a tree from the copse at the bottom of the hill and we'd all decorate it together on Christmas Eve, after Mum finished baking the mince pies. And in the evening, they'd let me put baby Jesus in the manger in the crib."

"You had a crib? How lovely."

"Yes, Dad made the stable out of offcuts of wood and some bits of cardboard. Then he glued straw in place for the thatched roof and across the floor. I made the figures out of papier-mâché when I was four. They got tatty as the years went on and every year Mum threatened to throw them out and buy new ones, but Dad and I argued so much that she gave in. 'Just one more year,' she'd say, 'and then they're going in the bin.' But we were still using them until the year she disappeared. And after that, we didn't seem to bother with a crib for ages. It's only the past couple of years I've resurrected the tradition. And I made a new set of figures, as we couldn't remember where the old ones had got to."

"Oh, that's a pity."

"Yes, it is. We found the old stable, but all the figures were missing. Even the special ones Dad had added to the collection."

"Special ones?"

"Well, although I could make the human figures successfully, I found it difficult to do the animals. Dad used to buy additional animals each year. He'd go to Christmas markets and craft fairs, looking especially for small animals. There were sheep and a tiny wooden lamb, a herd of plastic cattle, and even a stallion made of silver. We used to have him staring over the stall, gazing at the baby."

"And you don't know where they went to?"

"No, not at all. When we went to the attic to get everything out a few years back, we found the stable, but the box of figures was gone. We searched everywhere, but to no avail. So we've started a whole new collection. Dad goes out and buys an animal each year. And I search the internet to find something different." She giggled. "I bet we're the only family in the country where visitors to the baby Jesus include not only three wise men, the shepherds and their sheep, angels and archangels, but also a giraffe, a crocodile and an elephant."

"That's hilarious. I must see that when we get to December. And can I bring Suzy as well? She gets really excited at Christmas and just loves visiting people to see how they celebrate. We used to live in such a diverse community when we were in London. She saw many celebrations. I would hate her horizons to be reduced now we're living in the countryside."

Esther nodded her head.

"You and the rest of the family, will be more than welcome to come and visit the Fosters Farm Crib." She looked up at the clock on the shelf over the fireplace. "Goodness, you need to get back to work. Let me get this picture wrapped up for you."

CHAPTER 38

It took a bit of detective work, and that was what Rohan was good at, after all, but he tracked down Rory Black's father. Rohan arrived at the neat semi-detached house on the outskirts of Tamworth just after six pm. He'd learned that Jasper was a middle manager in a bank and therefore guessed he'd find him in by early evening.

"Mr Finch? Mr Jasper Finch?"

"Yes, that's me. What can I do for you?" The middle-aged man blinked at him through thick lenses, an uncertain smile on his face. Rohan pulled a card out of his pocket.

"I'm a private investigator, based in Devon. Could I have a word with you about a woman called Amelia Johnson? You would have known her as Amelia Wright?"

The man gave a start and then stepped back and gestured for Rohan to enter.

"That's a name I've not heard for a long time. You'd better come in, Mr Banerjee. This way." He pointed through the door into a neat front room, obviously used as the family lounge. There were books and tablets scattered across the coffee table and the television was showing a teatime games show, but with the sound muted. In the background, Rohan could hear youthful voices chatting. "My wife's giving the kids their supper," he went on, pointing towards the back of the house.

"Oh, I'm sorry, Mr Finch. Shall I come back at a more convenient time?" But Jasper Finch shook his head.

"No, this is fine. We let them get finished first, then we have ours later in peace while they're doing their homework. Although how much work actually gets done, we're never sure. You know what it's like with teenagers."

Not really, thought Rohan, but he smiled politely and nodded.

"How many children do you have, Mr Finch?"

"Three. Twin boys of sixteen and their little sister, who's eleven going on thirty." He paused and gestured for Rohan to sit down. "It was one reason my first marriage broke up. I've always wanted a family, and I thought Amelia felt the same way. At least, she led me to believe that was the case. We worked hard for a couple of years, saved lots of money, put down a deposit on a house. And then my elderly aunt died and left me all her money. So we paid off the mortgage. I was just setting up my business. Amelia persuaded me to put the house in her name. To protect it from the bank if the business went belly-up, she used to say. And I did. What an idiot."

"So what went wrong?"

"Well, everything changed once we got married. She made it quite clear she wouldn't be having any kids. She was much too interested in her career and her own happiness."

"How long did the marriage last?"

"Only nine months in total. She disappeared one day with no warning. I got back from work and she'd gone. And then, the following week, I found she'd sold the house without my knowledge. And taken all the money. I lost the business soon afterwards. Had to start all over again. It took me quite a long time to trust anyone after that, I can tell you." He paused and then looked at Rohan for the first time since he'd started this sorry tale. "Hmm, not sure why I told you all that. Must be hearing her name after so long. But tell me, Mr Banerjee. Why are you here? Why are you asking questions about Amelia? Is she in trouble?"

Rohan could see this man's first marriage hadn't been an easy one, and he was obviously open to the idea his former wife might be in trouble. But all the same, he'd always hated this part of the job. He cleared his throat.

"I'm afraid I have some bad news for you, Mr Finch."

Jasper Finch took the news of his former wife's death calmly. With sadness more than anything else. He was more distressed to hear he had a son, and that she'd not told him she was pregnant before she left.

"In fact, that's probably what triggered her leaving," Finch said reflectively. "She knew if she told me, I'd be all for keeping the child and trying to make a go of the marriage for his sake. Although, to be honest, I'm fairly certain she was cheating on me while she was still here, so I can't be certain the child is even mine."

"I suppose a DNA test would tell—" began Rohan, but Jasper Finch shook his head.

"No, I don't think so. You say she didn't put my name on this young man's birth certificate. And it looks like he's going to prison for a long time." He looked again towards the back of the house, where the laughter and banter were growing noisier by the minute. "I have my family here. Things are going well for me. I don't want to risk upsetting everything for a son I've never met."

Poor Rory Black, thought Rohan. *Someone else who doesn't want to know him or acknowledge any link to him.* He didn't condone murder, but he could understand why the young man had grown so bitter. He stood and held out his hand.

"Well, thank you for your time, Mr Finch. Again, I'm sorry to be the bearer of bad news. But thank you for filling in some of the background. That's been very helpful."

As the two men walked through the front hall, Finch's wife popped her head around the door of the dining room.

"The kids are just finishing, Jasper. Supper in ten, okay?" And she disappeared once again. Rohan stared after the woman with his mouth open. Tall and slim, with long red hair tumbling down below her shoulders. Jasper Finch obviously only went for one type of woman. Rohan glanced across at the other man, who was looking a tad sheepish.

"I know what you are thinking, Mr Banerjee. And yes, it was the looks that originally drew me to my wife, my second wife. But she was such a different person from Amelia. It was obvious I'd made a better choice the second time around."

As Rohan stood on the threshold, preparing to take his leave, Jasper Finch clutched at his arm.

"I want nothing to disrupt this marriage, Mr Banerjee. I'm sorry to hear Millie's dead, and even sorrier to hear how she died, but I don't think I'll be able to help you any further."

"Millie?"

"Oh yes. By the time we left, she was insisting everyone called her Amelia. But when I first met her, she was shy little Millie Wright, with no airs or graces at all. That's why I fell in love with her." He nodded at Rohan in a way that made him realise he would never see this man again. "Goodnight, Mr Banerjee." And the door closed softly but firmly, leaving Rohan standing in the empty driveway.

CHAPTER 39

"And I can't say I took to him, to be honest," said Rohan. He was sitting in Esther's kitchen the following afternoon, drinking fresh mint tea with Charlie and Annie. "He was a bit of a cold fish. Didn't want to have anything to do with poor Rory Black. Although I suppose you have to understand him not wanting anything to disrupt this second marriage. Life seems to be much better for him this time around."

"But don't forget 'poor Rory Black' as you call him bludgeoned a woman to death and then calmly crept away into the night," said Esther. "What do you think, Annie? Deserted child or hardened killer?" When there was no response, Esther reached over and nudged her guest, who was staring out of the window. "Earth to McLeod. Come in, McLeod."

Annie gave a start and then a little laugh.

"Sorry, Esther, did you say something?"

"It wasn't important. Where were you, anyway?"

"I was trying to remember something. Someone mentioned the name Millie or something similar, somewhere else recently."

"Someone who came into the pub, maybe?" asked Charlie. "Or someone who's made a booking for the future?"

Annie shook her head and wrinkled her brow.

"No, I don't think so. I don't think it was when I was at The Falls." She shrugged and stood up. "Never mind, I'm sure it'll come back to me. Right, we need to get going. I've got a bit more preparation to do for this evening's service. Then I want to nip down to The Folly and get Suzy's birthday presents wrapped before she gets back from school." She headed for the sink, empty mug in hand, then stopped and spun around on her toes, clicking her fingers at the same time. "That's it! I remember now. It was when I was here with you the other day, Esther. Do you remember telling me about the girls who used to come and help with the horses? And the one who was obsessed with your father?"

Esther laughed.

"Oh yes, of course. She used to come to the farm all dolled up and in full makeup, but with those big thick glasses and her long, mousy-coloured hair that was always greasy. But Dad took no notice of her. Then she fell in the mud one day and everyone laughed. I think that was the last time I saw her. It must have been in the March, just before my accident." She stopped and shook her head. "But I didn't think her name was Millie. I thought I called her Mollie. Or Polly even."

"No, I'm sure you called her Millie. I remember thinking it was such an old-fashioned name."

Charlie invited Rohan back to The Falls for an early supper, and he happily accepted. As they gathered their stuff together, ready to leave, Annie returned to the subject of the love-struck teenager, Millie. And her friend Catherine.

"Could you do a bit of digging, Rohan? See if you can track down those two young girls?" she asked.

"Why. What're you thinking?" asked Esther.

"Not sure. It might be nothing, but, as my gran used to say, my shoulders are tingling. Hearing the same name twice in a week seems just a little too much of a coincidence."

CHAPTER 40

The following day, Rohan phoned The Falls just after lunch and summoned Charlie and Annie to the farm. Esther had been baking again, so no-one argued with using her kitchen as investigation headquarters.

"You're right, Annie," he said. "It wasn't a coincidence. The girls' names were Millie Wright and Catherine Bromley. Catherine lived here in Coombesford, but went to school on the edge of Dartmoor. Millie came from Newton Abbot, and had spent no time in the countryside until she teamed up with Catherine at school. She came out to help her on Fosters Farm a few times. And apparently she took a shine to Tommy Steele and started following him around all the time. Even volunteered to help take the decorations down after Christmas one year.

Then one day she disappeared. But it was around the same time Esther had her accident and her mother June ran off, so no-one paid much attention to an awkward schoolgirl who was no longer around. Catherine reckons she went off to the Reading Festival and when she came back, she was all excited about some band member or other and lost all interest in the farm. The girls drifted apart soon after that."

"And what happened to them?"

"Well, Catherine's living in Chudleigh now. I went and had a chat with her this afternoon. She says Millie went on some training course in the Midlands and met someone while she was there. Got married soon afterwards, and they lost touch."

"Did she have an address or anything?"

"No, nothing like that. But she remembered one thing. Millie's fiancé's name was Jasper." Rohan opened his file and threw some papers on the table. "Meet Millie Wright, later to become Millie Finch. And finally, here is the marriage certificate for one Amelia Finch nee Wright and a James Johnson, who lives in Bristol. Mr Johnson confirms his wife was a stunning redhead who only hung around for a few months after they were married, before disappearing, having emptied the contents of their joint bank account. He also confirmed that before she disappeared he'd paid for private laser treatment on her eyes to correct her extreme short-sightedness."

CHAPTER 41

Celia was just emptying the teapot and shutting down the coffee machine for the evening when the bell over the door pinged. "I'm afraid we're closed," she said, looking up. But then her voice faded. It was those two detectives. DCI Harolds and DS Smith. What did they want? Not her Roger, surely? He'd assured her he'd had nothing to do with Stanley Wentworth's death.

The DCI smiled at Celia. She found that quite chilling.

"We're not here for coffee, Mrs Richardson. Although if you had any of those chocolate chip cookies left over..."

"Roger's not here," Celia whispered. "He's gone into Chudleigh."

But the DCI was shaking her head.

"It's you we want to talk to, Mrs Richardson. Please come and sit down."

Celia walked around from the back of the counter and across the café to the table by the door where the detectives had seated themselves. Her legs felt as if they were having difficulty moving in a straight line. She hoped she was going to make it. She collapsed into a third chair between the two of them. The DCI had a letter in her hand, which she placed on the table. Celia recognised the handwriting with a jolt and then realised her name was on the envelope.

"Mrs Richardson, Celia," said the DCI softly. "We've been searching the Village Store once again and we came across this letter addressed to you. It was in the office, slipped into one of the folders at the back of the filing cabinet. Do you recognise the handwriting?"

"Yes, I do." Celia nodded. "It's Stanley's."

"Really? That's very interesting. I understand you and Mr Wentworth used to be close?"

Celia nodded.

"Yes, we were engaged once. But that was such a long time ago. I was still a teenager."

"And did you renew your friendship when he returned to Coombesford a few years ago?"

"Certainly not!" Celia felt herself go hot and heard her voice rise up an octave. "You asked me that before! I know there were some rumours and my Roger got a silly idea into his head." She paused and took a deep breath, forcing herself to slow down and bring her voice back to normal, before carrying on more calmly. "But no, we never renewed our friendship, as you call it. In fact, quite the opposite. I told him it was far too late. And since then, Stanley, I mean Mr Wentworth, has made things difficult for us here at Cosy Corner. We've barely spoken since."

"Well, it would seem there was something he wanted to say to you, Celia." Harolds pushed the letter towards her. "It's addressed to you, so we haven't opened it. But I have to ask that you open it and read it here in front of us. And when you've done so, I may ask your permission to take the letter away as evidence if it can shed any light on Mr Wentworth's murder."

Celia lifted the envelope with trembling hands and opened it. There was a single sheet of paper in there, covered on both sides with Stanley's tiny neat writing. She took a deep breath and began to read. The letter was dated five weeks previously.

My dear Celia

For a long time now, I've owed you an explanation for why I ran away and left you standing at the altar. I know people think it was because I was in trouble with the law and ran away to escape capture. Well, I was in trouble, all right, but not exactly in the way you imagined.

1996. So long ago. And so many things happened that year. Young Esther had her accident on Chudleigh Rocks and was in a coma for months. Her mother disappeared and everyone reckoned she couldn't stand the thought of her daughter being crippled for life. Blamed herself for letting her go up on the rocks on her own. Pauline Wilson's father died suddenly. And we got engaged.

I doubt if you remember the two young girls who used to work with the horses up on the farm. Catherine and Millie, their names were. Catherine was a lovely young thing. I used to stop and talk to her when they were out riding the horses around the lanes. Her friend Millie was silent. I never took much notice of her, to be honest. Then one evening, she called out to me as I was walking through the fields. She was in a proper state, covered in mud, and she'd broken one lens in her glasses. I tried to find out what was wrong, but she wouldn't tell me to start with. She just kept saying she needed my help. Said there'd been an accident. She took me around to the back of one of the deserted barns and there was June Steele lying in the mud. Her horse had thrown her and rolled on her. It was obvious straight away there was nothing we could do for her. She was already dead. I said we had to call the ambulance and the police, tell Farmer Steele. But she just shook her head. Said it had been her fault. She'd put thistles under the horse's saddle to spook him and make him throw June. She said I had to help her hide the body so no-one would know what had happened, and they would think June had run away.

Of course, I refused. But then she pulled something out of her pocket. It was an article from a magazine, talking about people who were on the run. And there was a picture of me. It was the one the police had been using to try to find me. She said if I didn't help her, she'd report me to the police and I'd go to prison.

And, God forgive me, I agreed to help her. We hid the body in the old barn and she rode the horse back to the stable and cleaned him

159

down. It was the day after Pauline's dad's funeral, so that night, I took the body to the cemetery and buried it in the new grave.

Well, after that, we both kept quiet. I couldn't report her without implicating myself and likewise, she wouldn't say anything. Then, a few months later, she disappeared completely. Leaving me in the village where I'd buried a body and concealed a suspicious death. I couldn't stand the stress of it all. And I didn't want to start married life on that basis. Which is the real reason I ran away, Celia.

But the police caught up with me, anyway. And by the time I came back, it was too late. You'd married Roger. And yes, I realise it was my fault. But I want you to know I really loved you, Celia, and I just wish everything could have been different.

Yesterday, Pauline Wilson's mother died. I know that within a short while, they'll be opening her father's grave so the couple can finally reunite. But they're going to find more than just a coffin in that grave. Something tells me the entire story is going to come out. And if it does, I want to make sure you finally know the truth. So I'm writing this now. And if I'm arrested, I'll ask the police to give you this letter.

Just believe that I'm sorry, Celia, and that I never wanted to hurt you.

Yours ever
Stanley Wentworth

At that moment, the door opened and Roger breezed in.

"What's going on here then?" he asked.

Wiping her eyes with her hankie, Celia folded the letter and replaced it in the envelope. Then handing it to DCI Harolds, she nodded her head and, taking her husband's hand, headed towards the stairs and their little private haven.

CHAPTER 42

"But Stanley was killed, and he never got the chance to deliver the letter?" Annie asked. "How sad is that?"

Esther looked across at Charlie, and they exchanged a wry smile. Only soft-hearted Annie would feel sorry for the writer of that letter, despite everything he'd done and the effect his behaviour had had on both Celia and her own family. But there was one question that was still rankling with her.

"Do you think he knew Amelia was Millie?"

"No, I don't think so," said Charlie. "She'd remodelled herself, so she was unrecognisable. And if he had, he'd surely have mentioned it in the letter. And he wouldn't have employed her, surely? No, I guess he just thought he was about to be uncovered as the person who buried your mother's body. And was likely to be blamed for June's death as well."

"In which case, it would have been easy for her to get close to him and slip him the poison?"

"Yes, that's what the police think happened. They found the poison in Amelia's bathroom cabinet, although they didn't recognise what it was to begin with, and, as she was a murder victim herself, there was no reason to test it. Once I told DCI Harolds what her background was, they joined

161

all the dots, and it was quite easy to work out. They'd probably have got there on their own eventually, but they're very grateful for our help."

"So that leaves just one mystery to be solved," said Rohan, who looked as if he was about to burst if he didn't have his say. "And I've been saving this one till last."

"Roger?" asked Charlie.

"Got it in one. Roger's mysterious disappearances that had Celia so worried. I had a suspicion, and I got him to come clean the last time I saw him. But I bet you'll never guess what he's been up to."

The other three looked at him and his soppy grin. Finally, Esther could stand it no longer.

"Rohan Banerjee, if you don't tell us right now, I'm banning you from my kitchen!" She knew what a sweet tooth he had and how much he loved her cakes and biscuits.

"Singing!" Rohan said, flinging his arms wide. "He's been taking singing lessons from young Melanie." There was an immediate chorus of disbelief from his audience.

"Roger, singing?"

"No, I don't believe it."

"What on earth for?"

"It's true, I tell you. I checked with Melanie and she reluctantly admitted it. It's Celia's 45th later this year, and he's planning a surprise party for her. And he wants to serenade her during the evening."

"Well, I think it's a lovely idea. Good for him," said Annie. Then, standing up, she clapped her hands together.

"Right, guys. Suzy will be home in an hour and The Falls is going to be buzzing with eleven-year-olds. So it's all hands on deck! The place needs decorating. And I've got an entire load of balloons that need blowing up."

"Oh, but I've just got to…" began Rohan.

"And I need to help him…" said Charlie.

But Annie fixed them with a fierce stare and they meekly stood up, hugged Esther and headed for the door.

EPILOGUE

Esther was deep in the throes of planning her latest commission, an illustration for an online fantasy magazine, when a furious barking penetrated her concentration. Her own dog, Frisk, was in his usual position under the table, as close to her legs as he could get without actually lying across them. He pulled himself to his feet and lumbered across the room in the direction of the noise.

It surprised Esther to see long shadows surrounding her, and she looked at her watch. Nearly eight o'clock! Where on earth had the rest of the afternoon gone? Once Charlie, Annie, and Rohan had left, she'd come in here for a few minutes while waiting for her father to return home. The evening's supper was ready, and she'd wanted to jot a few ideas down while they were fresh in her mind. But, as often happened, she'd got completely absorbed.

But nearly eight o'clock. Where on earth was her father? And what was going on out in the farmyard? The barking continued, getting louder all the time. Esther hurried into the kitchen and looked out of the window.

A young black and white sheepdog was running round in circles, excitedly barking. It was Tinker, her father's dog. When he saw Esther he threw himself at the door, ran back to the gate, then back to the door once more.

Esther looked across the fields and down into the valley. Her father's old Land Rover sat next to the long barn where they stored all the winter feed for the cattle. But there was no sign of him. Then, with a cry of dismay, she saw a plume of smoke rising from the back of the barn. And as she watched, a long gout of flame rose amid the smoke.

If her father's vehicle was down there, so was he. And if she couldn't see him, chances were he was inside the barn. But, at this time of night, all the farmhands had gone home. She was on her own. Then a thought hit her. The horses! The three thoroughbreds stabled at Fosters Farm normally stayed in the brand new block on the other side of the farmhouse. But there was a problem with drainage and her father had moved them temporarily into the stalls in the old barn while the repairs were being done.

"Frisk, stay," she yelled, pointing to his bed in the corner. Then, without waiting to see if he obeyed, Esther Steele opened the kitchen door. Tinker threw himself into her arms.

"Good boy," she said, patting his head. He raced back towards the gate and stood waiting for her, his bark quieter now, but no less insistent. Esther stepped over the threshold and began running.

As she thudded through the gate and into the field, she was vaguely aware of a black and white shape racing past her. Tinker was soon half a field away, dashing down the hill towards the blazing building and his master. Every so often he paused and looked over his shoulder, as if to check she was still on his tail.

At first, the barn seemed rather to recede into the distance. But gradually it grew in size as she approached. She smelled burning wood and straw. The front of the barn was still untouched, but the back was fully ablaze now and in the distance she could hear creaking timbers above the roar of the flames.

Without slowing her stride, she pulled up the scarf from around her neck and used it to cover her mouth. Reaching

164

the barn, she glanced to one side and was relieved to see tall shapes in the distance. At least the horses were out. Although she could only see two of them. She prayed the third one was around the corner, out of sight. But then she heard a squeal from inside and realised her prayer was unanswered.

Eyes watering, she ran through the open barn door and stopped in horror. Majesty, the black thoroughbred in the furthest stall, was kicking at the door, eyes rolling in terror. Then she spotted her father, lying face down on the ground in front of the stall. A smouldering upright had fallen across his shoulders and although the flames hadn't yet reached him, it was only a matter of time. Tinker was running around in circles near his fallen master.

With a yell, Esther raced across the barn, and grabbed the untouched end of the upright. It was unwieldy, but not heavy. It must have hit Tommy Steele from behind and knocked him out. Esther pulled hard and cleared the post off her father. Then grabbing him by his shoulders, she dragged him clear of the barn, all the time calling soothingly to the terrified horse.

Reaching the Land Rover, she gently lowered her father back onto the ground. "Stay, Tinker," she said to the young dog, who with a whine collapsed onto his belly and crawled towards his unconscious master, resting his nose on the farmer's chest.

Esther took a couple of deep breaths, pulled the scarf more tightly across her face, and ran back into the barn. The flames were spreading even faster now and the stall next to Majesty's was already alight. She pulled on the bolt, but it refused to move. Trying to ignore the increasingly hysterical noises from the enormous horse, she grabbed a block of wood from the corner of the barn and rammed it against the bolt. Once, twice, three times, nothing happened. But on the fourth go, it finally gave. The bolt shot out, the stall door flew open, and Majesty was free; out of the stall, out of the barn, and across the field toward his stablemates.

With a sob, Esther quickly checked there was no-one else in the building and then ran for the door.

As she struggled to catch her breath, she threw herself to the ground next to her father. Her hands were throbbing. She tried to take a deep breath, but that only made her cough and splutter more. She felt herself slipping away.

It was Tinker who brought her back to herself. His whines were becoming increasingly frantic, interspersed with an occasional insistent yipping sound.

Her father! She needed to get help. Jumping to her feet, she stifled her coughs and bent over to gaze at his face. What she saw made her blood run cold. There was a large gash on the side of his head, from which blood was still oozing. In stark contrast to the bright red, the farmer himself was chalky white. He appeared to have lost a huge amount of blood. For one long horrified moment, she thought he was not breathing. But a faint flutter of his eyelids told her he was still alive.

Esther reached into her pocket for her phone. Chills ran down her spine as she realised she didn't have it with her. She was alone in a field half a mile from the farmhouse, with her seriously injured father and no-one within hailing distance. She considered running back to the house, but didn't think her legs or her lungs would carry her all that way. And she was reluctant to leave her father alone, injured like this.

There was only one thing for it. Help wouldn't come to him. She would have to drive him to help instead.

Esther's father was not a small man and, unconscious, he was a dead weight, but from somewhere, she found the strength to drag him up into the back of the Land Rover. Grabbing the emergency blanket he always kept under the front seat, she formed a pillow for his head and made him as comfortable as she could. Tinker jumped in after them and wedged himself against his master, licking his hand.

"Protect, Tinker," she said, climbing out of the back of the vehicle and closing the door. Racing to the front, she pulled open the driver's door, whispering a prayer to herself that the keys would be in the ignition. And this time, someone answered her prayer. Slamming the door, she closed her eyes, took a deep breath, and turned the ignition key.

Esther had rarely left her home for the past twenty-odd years. But her father had insisted on teaching her to drive, and she'd practised in the farmyard on her good days, once everyone had gone home.

The Land Rover was an automatic. She pulled the handle into Drive, released the handbrake and slammed her foot down on the accelerator. The vehicle surged forward towards the burning barn. Esther screamed, lifted her foot off the pedal, pushed hard on the brake and clung to the steering wheel as the vehicle shuddered to a halt. In the back of the vehicle, Tinker gave a louder than usual whine.

"It's okay, boy, it's okay," she said. Then, taking a deep breath, she slipped the lever to Reverse and gently applied pressure to the accelerator. The vehicle crawled backward, away from the barn. She turned the wheel gently and was relieved to feel herself move in a circle. Inching it around, she finally faced uphill. The fire gave off an orange glow which reflected in the rear-view mirror. Looking over her shoulder, she saw the light illuminating the unmoving figure of her father and his young sheepdog.

Esther took a deep breath, put the vehicle back into Drive, and lifted her foot off the brake. As they moved forward and climbed the hill she gradually gained in confidence, and by the time she reached the top gate, she was flying across the ground. She only just remembered to slam the brakes on before she shot out of the gate and into the lane. She turned left, gasping as the side of the vehicle grated along the gatepost. Then, with a bump and a shudder, they were out on the lane and moving away from the farm and towards the village. Esther hadn't stopped to switch on the headlights, and she prayed they wouldn't meet anyone in the narrow lane. Once again, the fates were with her.

Within seconds, and without meeting another vehicle, she was out of the lane and on the junction with the main road, facing the village green.

To her left, she could see the school and Cosy Corner, both in darkness. Opposite was the church and the vicarage. But to her right, she could just see The Falls, her friends' pub and, to her relief, there was light spilling from every window. Wrenching the steering wheel around, she drove across the road and into the car park. Not stopping to park, she jumped from the cab and raced to the front door. Bursting through, she barely registered the crowded bar, or the shocked looks on the drinkers' faces. Seeing Charlie and Annie behind the bar, she opened her mouth, but no words came out. Sinking to the ground, she felt everything spin. Hands grabbed her.

"Outside. In the Land Rover. My father. Help him," she wheezed. Momentarily, everything went black.

"Charlie, call an ambulance!" she heard someone shout. Annie put her arm around the dazed woman, helped her to her feet, and walked her over to the nearest table. Outside, through the window, she could see a crowd gathered around the back of the Land Rover. Then the front door opened and Roger Richardson walked in, bent over and holding on with difficulty to Tinker's collar. The dog was struggling to get away.

"Can someone look after this youngster?" he called. "We're trying to help Tommy, and it doesn't help to have an agitated pup running around under our feet."

Esther roused herself and called out weakly: "Tinker, heel, come here."

The young dog stopped running in circles, looked at Esther, looked back at the doorway and then, as though recognising everything was under control, meekly trotted over to the table and curled up at her feet. "Good dog," she said, rubbing his back, "wonderful dog." She looked up at Annie with tears stinging her already sore eyes. "Tinker probably saved my dad's life," she said. "If it wasn't for him,

I'd never have seen the fire in the barn until it was far too late."

"Barn? Fire? Esther, what are you talking about?" But Esther closed her eyes and drifted off. Explanations were just too difficult at the moment.

When the ambulance arrived, Esther was told her dad had regained consciousness and was going to be all right, although he reluctantly agreed to go to the hospital for a check-up because of the blow to his head. Apparently, he'd not lost as much blood as she'd thought.

"And you need to go in the ambulance with your dad," said Annie. "You need checking out, too. We can park the Land Rover safely for you overnight."

"Yes, that would be good," said Esther. "Someone can come and fetch it in the morning."

Suddenly, with the immediate emergency over, Esther realised what a strange situation this was. For the first time, she was sitting in the bar of The Falls all by herself. She began to laugh.

"Esther, are you okay?"

"I certainly am, Annie. Everything is just perfect. I was so concerned about my dad and getting him to safety, I didn't stop to think what I was doing. For the first time since childhood, I've left the confines of my home on my own. And you know what? I feel fine!"

"Do you mean you're cured?" someone asked.

"Not sure about cured. I'm sure when I calm down, I'm going to realise how scary all this has been. And I'll probably panic. But, I definitely think this is the beginning of a new phase. I reckon things are going to be very different from now on for the Steeles of Fosters Farm."

ENJOYED THIS BOOK?

Reviews and recommendations are very important to an author and help contribute to a book's success. If you have enjoyed *Villainy at the Village Store* please recommend it to a friend, or better still, buy them a copy for their birthday or Christmas. And please consider posting a review on your preferred review site.

ACKNOWLEDGMENTS

I am once again very grateful for all the support provided by my friends in the thriving community of writers and readers, both in Devon and beyond.

In particular, my thanks go to Carol Amorosi who moved from the role of beta reader to writing buddy this time around; to my friends in Chudleigh Writers' Circle and Exeter Writers; and to Margaret Barnes, Jenny Benjamin, Clare Lillington, Heather Morgan and Richard Morgan, my wonderfully inciteful beta readers.

Berni Stevens (@circleoflebanon) is responsible, as always, for the beautiful cover and Otis Lea-Weston continues to develop the map of Coombesford. Julia Gibbs (@ProofreadJulia) made sure the final text is as error-free as possible. My thanks go to all of them.

I owe a huge debt of gratitude to my sisters, Margaret Andow and Sheila Pearson, for their analytical reading skills and ongoing cheerleading.

Finally, my thanks go, as always, to my husband Michael McCormick, my fiercest critic and strongest supporter, who read this manuscript at least four times before I got it right.

ABOUT THE AUTHOR

Elizabeth Ducie was born and brought up in Birmingham. As a teenager, essays and poetry won her an overseas trip via a newspaper competition. Despite this, she took scientific and business qualifications and spent more than thirty years as a manufacturing consultant, business owner and technical writer before returning to creative writing in 2006. She has written short stories and poetry for competitions—and has had a few wins, several honourable mentions and some short-listing. She is published in several anthologies.

Under the Chudleigh Phoenix Publications imprint, she has published, in addition to her novels, two collections of short stories and co-authored another two. She also writes non-fiction, including *The Business of Writing* series for writers running their own small business. Her debut novel, *Gorgito's Ice Rink*, was runner-up in the 2015 Self-Published Book of the Year awards. The first in the Suzanne Jones series, *Counterfeit!*, came third in the 2015 Literature Works First Page Writing Prize.

Elizabeth is editor of the Chudleigh Phoenix Community Magazine, and a member of Chudleigh Writers' Circle and Exeter Writers.

For more information on Elizabeth, visit her website: www.elizabethducie.co.uk; follow her on Goodreads, Facebook, Twitter or Pinterest; or watch the trailers for her books on YouTube. To keep up to date with her writing plans, and for a monthly free short story, subscribe to her email list: elizabeth@elizabethducie.co.uk

OTHER BOOKS BY ELIZABETH DUCIE

Coombesford Books
Murder at Mountjoy Manor
Coombesford Calendar volume I

The Suzanne Jones series:
Counterfeit!
Deception!
Corruption!

Other fiction:
Gorgito's Ice Rink
Flashing on the Riviera
Parcels in the Rain and Other Writing

Co-written with Sharon Cook:
Life is Not a Trifling Affair
Life is Not a Bed of Roses

Non-fiction:
Sunshine and Sausages

The Business of Writing series:
Part 1: Business Start-Up (ebook only)
Part 2: Finance Matters (ebook only)
Part 3: Improving Effectiveness (ebook only)
Parts 1-3 (print only)
Parts 1-3 Workbook (print only)
Part 4: Independent Publishing